Read about Bahar's gripping and redemptive past in this **FREE, award-semi-finalist story.**

For the latest book news, sign up at

amyearls.com/behind-walls/.

PRAISE FOR UNDER HIS WINGS SERIES

Meadow's Curse is a beautifully woven portal fantasy that will sweep readers into a world of adventure, romance, and deep spiritual themes. Amy Earls crafts a tale that will intrigue fantasy fans and readers of faith alike. A thought-provoking reimagining of one of the Bible's most cherished love stories.

— LINDSAY A. FRANKLIN, CAROL AWARD-WINNING AUTHOR OF *THE STORY PEDDLER*

Meadow's Curse is a fantastically romantic finish to the *Under His Wings* series. Pero must wrangle with storms, lost love, and broken relationships as she meddles with the past and alters her future. But more important than the finish are the lessons along the way and leaning into the One who holds her heart. Open *Meadow's Curse* expecting to be entertained and leave satisfied with a deeper appreciation for God—the One who holds your heart, too.

— J F ROGERS, AUTHOR OF *THE CURSED LANDS* TRILOGY

Amy Earls crafts tales that are epic and unexpected, carefully weaving both faith and fantasy into narratives that are sure to thrill teen readers!

— LAUREN H. BRANDENBURG, MULTI-AWARD WINNING AUTHOR OF *THE DEATH OF MUNGO BLACKWELL*

Amy Earls' prose is vivid and witty, portraying a stunning world and complex emotions with equal skill and always finding room for a dash of humor where appropriate. I recommend this book to all.

— LEXIE FOX, READERS' FAVORITE 5-STAR REVIEW

Christian fantasy at its finest. I cannot recommend this book enough.

— VALICITY ELAINE, AUTHOR OF *BEAUTIFUL LIES*

Perfect for fans of Christian speculative fiction!

— KAREN GRUNST, AUTHOR OF *THE SACRED FIRE SAGA*

MEADOW'S CURSE

UNDER HIS WINGS BOOK 3

AMY EARLS

PORTAL
PUBLICATIONS

ISBN 979-8-9927926-0-7 (hardback)
ISBN 979-8-9874017-9-8 (paperback)
ISBN 979-8-9874017-8-1 (ebook)
ISBN 979-8-9927926-1-4 (audiobook)

Cover design by Seventhstar Art, www.SeventhStarArt.com

Find out more at www.AmyEarls.com

BOOKS BY AMY EARLS

Under His Wings series

Behind Walls (prequel)

The King's Feather (Book 1)

Forbidden Reign (Book 2)

Meadow's Curse (Book 3)

For Yeshua.
Your love story is the greatest ever written.
Thank you for inviting me to be in it.

May you be richly rewarded by the Lord, the God of
Israel, under whose wings you have come to take refuge.

— BOAZ, SON OF SALMON & RAHAB

You and I stargazing
Intertwining souls
We were never strangers
You were right there all along

— MYLES SMITH

PROLOGUE

GREEN MEADOW TIMES

February 24, 2026

Local Weather Forecaster Urges Immediate Evacuation

In a dramatic turn of events, Green Meadow's trusted weather forecaster, Steven Wayne, has issued an urgent plea for residents to evacuate immediately due to rapidly deteriorating weather conditions. The move may not come as a shock to the community, as many have already fled Oregon's town after last week's high winds destroyed hundreds of homes.

Wayne, known to be meticulously accurate with details, held a press conference early this morning to share the alarming forecast. "I have never seen such a rapid escalation in weather conditions," he stated. "Unfortunately, forecasters predict this as the beginning of the negative effects these storms will cause. It is imperative that we take immediate action to ensure the safety of our town."

Through the use of innovative robotics, including drones and Enhanced Radar Technology, the forecast includes predictions of earthquakes, high-speed winds, and the possibility of tornadoes. Wayne warned these conditions could result in widespread damage to property and pose a significant risk to human life. "The safety of our residents is my top priority," he asserted.

As Green Meadow faces this unprecedented weather emergency, unity and cooperation are more important than ever. Wayne's urgent warning serves as a stark reminder of the unpredictable nature of weather and the need for preparedness and attentiveness.

1

DREAM

SAM

Green Meadow, Oregon
March 26, 2026

I *am immortal.*

That's what I should've said to the anchorwoman on OBC news in this morning's Zoom interview.

"How has the hazardous weather not affected your streaming services?" Monica asks.

From my living room couch, I watch the replay of the recording on my phone, the only electronic device with some remaining battery after today's interview. The screen moves from Monica's scrunched forehead to my lifted brows. I'm not proud of the next line and cringe when I hear my voice.

"I suppose being evicted from one's home means nothing compared to working technology."

Monica nods her head. "My apologies for the insensitive question, Mr. Nesim."

I lean forward, bringing my face closer to the camera. Has my nose always looked so pronounced? "Apology accepted.

And, please, call me Sam." I sound like some celebrity looking for a hot date.

"*Sam*, I'm not only speaking for myself when I wish for you to be safe like the rest of Green Meadow's citizens currently are."

Was that an eye roll? I thought I'd kept that to myself. Good grief. Did I show *any* civility for the interview?

Monica clears her throat as if she needs to remove fake tears before speaking. "For those of you just tuning in, a small town in Oregon's Willamette Valley has been in turmoil from a bout of unprecedented weather that has slowly increased in intensity over the year. So far, this incremental weather pattern only impacts within Green Meadow's borders. In fact, those who live outside of the county's perimeters are left unscathed."

I flinch, my heart slamming against my ribs. That's where I should be, outside of this living nightmare. OBC shows a quick shot of people lined up across the edge of the border. An invisible wall hovering in the air keeps them dry while the storm rages on the other side. A few extend their hands across the edge, then bring them back wet.

"Last week," Monica continues, "those who heeded weather forecaster Steven Wayne's suggestion for immediate evacuation from Green Meadow are safe while others like Sam Nesim, who I'm speaking with now, refused to leave. As of five days ago, after the town's evacuation, another forecasted event of severe weather swept through Green Meadow, killing at least twelve people who remained in the once thriving rural town."

I'm ready for her to snap at me about ignoring the forecaster's warning, how I'm throwing my life on the line. Instead, she proceeds with the facts.

"Of the fifty thousand drones which monitored the latest conditions in Green Meadow, the fierce wind storms have left seven thousand, hindering information on survivors of the predicted weather catastrophes. The remaining found survivor is Sam Nesim, who remarkably still has communication access to our news team." Monica pauses for a second, then plunges into her next question. "I think what we Oregonians, as well as the entire American population, really want to hear is, when do you plan on leaving?"

There it is. As I slouch back against the cushion, I brace myself for my approaching answer to her question. Its lingering impact once again takes my breath away.

What am I thinking by staying here? And how am I still alive? I press my forehead into my fingers and rub hard. My brain must be missing something important, yet I can't shake the thought loose.

"I'm not leaving." I hear myself say the words from this morning's interview, and still it shocks me as much as it seems to stun Monica.

"Others stayed put because of their land or the comfort of their home. Can I assume, Sam, that you won't leave for one of those reasons?"

On the screen, I shake my head, a visible swallow sliding down my throat. "I stay because my God told me to."

"The weather predictions show more storms for Green Meadow. Will you not move, even if it means you won't make it?"

"I won't die."

"How can you be sure, Sam?" Monica leans in without a single glance at herself on her Zoom screen.

"I don't think I can."

"Did I hear you say you don't think you can die?" Her lips form a thin line, failing to match my confidence. Or is that a snicker she's hiding?

"You are correct."

"What about this last hit? Wind threw whole houses across the town, including part of your kitchen."

I look at the large hole in my kitchen wall. No use trying to fix it when the next storm will knock it back down. Currently, it's peaceful outside. Is it a trick of the light or did some creature crawl through the opening? I squint, but without spotting any trace of movement. No matter. Let the lizards join me. What's left of my house is a better alternative than staying outside in the elements.

"Are you not afraid you'll be next?" Monica asks from my phone.

"Oh, I'm terrified, but I don't think it will kill me because Elohim's protecting me in order to fulfill His mission. I have the solution to stopping the storms."

Monica's eyes widen. "Please, Sam, if you have a solution, don't refrain. The whole world is listening."

I shake my head. The world won't like what they hear next. Not when they hardly grasped why I stayed put. Choosing to live in the heart of a severe weather warning is one thing, but to confess I hold the secret formula to stop the storm is another.

"The chosen," I hear myself say from the screen.

"Excuse me," Monica replies, "but did you say, 'the chosen?'"

I give one brief nod. "There are three chosen. One named Bahar said *yes* when Elohim asked her to marry a man named Salmon, and the result was me. When Elohim asked me to plant a garden, I accepted. Even when the ground became cursed, I felt the conviction to stay. But bringing life to this place is not something I can do alone; I wait for help from an unforgettable woman, whom I hope to marry."

Monica's smirk tells me she's amused by the conversation but doesn't believe a word I say. "And who is this woman?"

My shy smile and shimmering eyes show what I thought my heart kept secret. "Her name is Ruth."

"Let me get this straight, Sam. You're battling fierce winds, rain, floods, and earthquakes, ultimately endangering yourself for a girl."

"Not just a girl."

Monica nods. "Yes, I know. An unforgettable woman named Ruth. Where will you find this woman? How do you know she's alive?"

The corner of my mouth twitches as I watch the replay, knowing my next line. "She's alive in my dreams nightly, though this might sound unrealistic, so let me clarify. She lives in a galaxy far, far away."

With a hearty laugh, I recline against the couch. Despite its cliché, I still like that line. It wasn't like Monica would've believed me if I'd told her Pero Ruth came from another planet called Origo, where she stayed after her trip to China to be near family. My Star Wars answer alone stumped Monica.

My phone's battery dies. There goes the last of technology for the unseeable future. I plug the phone into its charger, just in case some miracle happens. Standing, I stretch with a groan. Before tonight's expected storm, I should take my eagle Faith to visit a deserted store for more bottled water. I could use a couple canned veggies, too. No power in this town as of three days ago, so I can't rely on refrigerated food or microwavable dinners. At least I can survive for a short period. Since I've confirmed how crazy I am to the reporters, I'm certain they'll leave me alone to die. Scratch that, to *live*.

I pinch my arm and feel the sting, yet I haven't seen a single injury from the episodes that have blown through Green Meadow. I'm still alive, though I've had plenty of opportunity to be hurt.

Heat throbs in my blood. I don't want to wait anymore. I don't want to hear *not yet*. But I can't cause Elohim's approval any more than I can cease the thunder's tremor during the long nights. If it's not according to His purpose, I'll stay.

Yet, I won't stop knocking on God's door.

"Can I ask her now, Creator?" I can't deny the longing in my voice, the strain I hope brings the answer I seek.

I am an Eve-less Adam, cultivating a farm that doesn't produce; a land that won't show mercy.

Perhaps I'm not immortal, but I *am* unmistakably and miserably alone.

Now.

Elohim's voice comes as a whisper in my heart, and with it, an extra beat of hope.

I quickly grab paper and pen from the living room desk. Pausing, I stare at the pen, suddenly aware that Pero could read my words as inviting, or push them away indefinitely.

With a heavy sigh and trembling hand, I start.

Dear Pero.

Hovering pen over paper, I plan my next line.

2

SEEK

SAM

Dear Pero,

A tree's scream isn't shrill. It's deeper, like roots. Like a wolf's growl before he attacks, a sound echoing desperation.

At night, when I lie in my bed awake, I hear the trees scream. It terrifies me I have the gift of growing nature, but I cannot control who she becomes.

Remember when you could hear leaves gently sway in the breeze? Remember when Green Meadow was green? I imagine what it must've been like when you lived here: lush fields to run through, birds singing sweet songs. But all signs of life have flown away. The local weather forecaster says the change is from extreme weather conditions, but something else is happening. This will sound strange, but I think that creation is calling to me for help. But I cannot help her. I wish to. A deep desire has settled inside me, like I cannot rest until I take care of Elohim's creation.

And so, I stay.

You probably heard that Dr. Carper (your bio dad—so

strange to say) left as well. The sanctuary he was planning on being king of in Green Meadow was vacated. He offered to fly me along with him to China. From his perspective, the sanctuary Dr. Henry Beggs attends in Beijing has expanded and is flourishing. I could live comfortably elsewhere, yet I remain committed to this land. It's hard to explain, Pero. I feel called here, like the land urges me to stay.

I ask the same question every day. "How long, Creator?" Gazing at the sky, I sense Elohim hiding beyond a painted ceiling. The sky also cries, dropping tears without pause. Elohim isn't in the sky. He's beyond all of this. So far above it all that I wonder where He's gone.

Pero, can you hear me call from the other universe? I open doors and closets, I approach swaying trees in the forest, and I ask them "How long?" as if the question will open a door for me to enter and find you. The sky's tears respond, yet never soften the soil. Hard dirt reaps hard dirt. Gazing at the sky, I sense Elohim hiding beyond a painted ceiling. Without a beginning, we have no birds, no wine, insects, honeybees, seasons, fresh food. No life.

I'm this town's last resident. Those remaining were swept up in tornadoes and earthquakes. It's as if creation pushed out all life. Each morning, I walk past a ruined house, finding no one there. I am like Noah, the last man standing after a fierce flood.

My supplies will soon vanish, mirroring the town, yet it seems I'll be here through it all. Elohim preserves me.

For three years, my hands have struggled against the unforgiving earth. I have nothing. I make nothing. Only the trees and I live.

Then there is you, Ruth.

Tell me if you're not okay with me calling you by your birth name. Ever since I learned Alexis is your biological mother, I can't get "Ruth" out of my head. Perhaps it's because of my promise to protect you all those years ago. I still intend to keep my promise. No matter how many worlds a part we are or if you prefer to be called Ruth or Pero, you will always be a treasure.

I've asked Faith to deliver letters to Alexis these last five years (only about a year long for me on Earth), and I trust Alexis has passed on my "hello" and "how are you". I haven't written because, well, I don't want you thinking I'm trying to propose or anything. In fact, can we start over as friends? Can I also get personal and say that I'm sorry about your breakup with Henry? It's been five years for you, about ten months for me. Yet I still miss my best friend, and I can imagine you more so. Pluck a feather from Faith when you see her, if it gives you any bit of comfort. Hug our moms for me.

So. After years of no letter from me to you, why am I writing now? Frankly, I could use your help. The property inherited from Jimmy has been damaged beyond repair, and the soil is immovable, as you know. I can no longer plant. The harvest has shriveled. And I can't return to Origo—to you—without a door opening. But if a door opens for you, we could turn around this storm. You see, I believe Elohim has allowed a curse on Green Meadow. I inexplicably heard Elohim repeat the words that He said to the first man: "cursed is the ground." Based on the increase of recent natural disasters, I believe it was His voice.

Cursed is the ground; blessed are the chosen. And perhaps we, chosen for this moment, will bring Elohim's redemption to the broken land.

I understand if you say no. If I didn't feel called to be here, I'd join you all immediately. I'd be gleaning on Shea's wisdom, getting to know my birth mom, relishing laughter and love from the best Lesarien family I've ever known. However, I've learned that this place of solitude hasn't been as lonely as expected, but as water is to a thirsty soul. I've consumed Elohim's healing of my past, arriving at a total dependence on Him. My very existence is at His mercy. Yet these storms disrupt my solitude, pushing me elsewhere. A new season. Perhaps that involves you. Oh, how I pray it does!

Am I too bold? Please don't turn away from my words. You have an irreplaceable gift, and I think your voice and guitar would calm the largest of storms. I'm worried I'm being greedy and demanding too much.

Creation is alive, and every day, she's louder. She lacks your song, Ruth. Would you come sing to her? I'm not sure how much longer I can stay here without a change.

Please pray. If we ever needed Elohim to bring His Kingdom here on Earth, it is now. The coming Messiah will change everything.

Yours Ever,
Sam

3

FEAR

PERO

Origo
April 17, 2030

"Pero."

A breeze whispers my name like it has every night. I squint, looking for a source, but the sting against my face forces my eyes closed.

The wind picks up speed, swirling my hair. I don't run. Instead, I steady my feet on the dry grass and call against the whooshing roar. "What do you want?"

My voice is swallowed, yet my body remains steadfast. I will not let nature seize me. I will stay and fight.

When the air settles into a steady sway, I survey the deserted town. Buildings are demolished, cars are smashed and tossed along the roads, and streets are empty.

A figure emerges in the distance, drawing toward me. I stand still. No longer do I hide from fear and uncertainty. Whoever or whatever comes my way has something for me. Maybe I won't like it, and perhaps I'll say no to whatever it is they offer. But I will not be afraid. Elohim is with me and will fight for me.

Each night's dream ends here, and I anticipate waking up any moment now. A woman's silhouette is near. Her pace is purposeful, brisk, yet unhurried.

The breeze carries her voice to me. "Sing."

I swallow hard. Many nights, the Lesaries have sung to Elohim, and I have joined them. Lately, I've led His people into songs of celebration and joy, evoking memories of releasing the Lesaries from Beijing's Forbidden City into Origo.

"Who are you?"

The figure disappears in a flash, and I reach forward, wishing I could take back what I'd said.

"Wait!" My extended arm falls to my side. "Why should I sing?"

Go.

Elohim's voice in my mind resounds like an echo.

I gasp as the world fades from view.

A GASP FILLS THE AIR. I blink in light and recognize the sound as my own. The entrance to my tent flaps open, revealing a bright sky and sticky air waking me with another sauna-like morning. Sweat lines my shirt. I close the tent tight and change into the only other shirt I own. Months ago, I threw out the yoga pants and jeans and replaced them with billowing cotton trousers, the same type I once thought humorous on Sam with his green flannel, button-down shirt. No longer do I care if my two tanks clash with the Middle Eastern style trousers. We aren't in Hollywood. This is Lesaries' country. Wilderness Highway. Survival of the fittest, not the sexiest.

Laying down on my mat, I pick the crust out of my eyes and yawn. Another dream. They are becoming more frequent. At first, I dreamed of Sam calling my name. Then, a distant figure emerges. But who is it?

I groan, then force myself up to standing. Now's the ideal moment to ask Shea, before the camp wakes. I chew on a crushed mint leaf and swallow water from my canteen. Oh, how I miss toothpaste! Several things I've learned to live without and most I don't miss at all, such as my phone or internet. I still miss toiletries. Occasionally, an eagle delivers supplies for Earth. Many are addressed from Henry or Sam, but distributing limited soap to tens of thousands of people is nearly impossible.

I'm not about to complain, though. Elohim has supplied us with plenty of food from heaven and water from rocks. We are well provided for.

I pull on my running shoes, or what's left of them. The Nike swish disappeared earlier this year, and the hole in the front nearly exposes my big toe. It's better than the sandals most Lesaries wear, with loose straps securing their feet against leather. If I were in America right now, I'd buy shoes for everyone.

The first rays of sun cast over the horizon when I step outside. In Origo, nothing in nature changes—no thunder, no lightning, no breeze to cool down flushed faces. A few early risers sit by their own shelters to watch the only scenery worth watching any more. Origo remains a barren land with no rain to bring color and no wildlife to roam. Yet the light is wonderful.

Today's show displays a horizontal, vibrant red with pink tones layered above. Taking in a sharp breath, I let it out. *Thank you for this day, Elohim. I choose to be happy in it.*

Around me, thousands of tents stretch on, like an endless array of Elohim's people. Scanning the premises, I find Shea at the top of a hill, pacing while in prayer. I rarely wake early enough to see him, but on the mornings after a vivid dream, I join him. There are moments we stay quiet, lost in our own prayers. When I sense it is an okay moment, I ask him questions about Elohim, and he answers with enough wisdom to have me pondering deep thoughts for days.

Shea places his large hand against a tree. As I near it, I shuffle my feet along the dirt so he's aware of my presence. He doesn't say a thing, but I sense he's heard me as he nods his head.

I go around the tree trunk and sit, leaning against the bark. I exhale and close my eyes, opening them when Shea lowers himself to sit on a fallen log. He isn't as quick these days and releases a slight grunt, as if it pained him to bend toward the ground.

"Don't forget to inhale." His voice is deep and strong.

I breathe in the calming tone. "You know." I clear my throat. "Most American therapists would say the opposite."

His gaze never leaves the view ahead. "What do you notice when you inhale?"

"Thousands of sweaty bodies. Dirt in my nose."

"What else?"

He asks me this when I am to search deeper. So, I dig for the answers that lie beneath the surface. "When you speak, I feel calm, but my voice is still scratchy from the morning. A little weak."

"Good. And what does that mean?"

"That you are a morning person, and I'm not." My chuckle fades when he doesn't smile.

"Try again."

"That meditating with Elohim strengthens you, while dwelling on trivial things such as toothpaste makes me weak."

"You're looking within yourself for the answers, but if what you've inhaled isn't true, you won't find direction there. First, ask yourself, what can you learn about Elohim?"

I scrunch my brows. "Wouldn't it make more sense to learn *from* Elohim?"

"Learning *about* Him really is learning *from* Him when you learn from *here*." He places a hand on his heart.

"I still don't understand."

"Don't try to know, Pero. Inhale, and you will taste His goodness."

"Should I ever exhale for this exercise?"

"You will understand how to breathe out once you learn to breathe in."

"Always speaking in riddles."

Shea turns his head toward the tents and frowns.

"What's wrong?"

He has aged in the last five years with more white strands of hair. The twinkle that once sparkled in his eye has dimmed. He used to exude joy and steadfastness, and although he is still faithful to lead the Lesaries and pray, I sense weariness in his voice and concern in his wrinkled brow.

"Elohim showed me more battles, more lands to claim." He shakes his head. "If you haven't noticed, I'm getting older."

"Nah. You can't be much older than Carper."

Shea grins. "You're kind, Pero."

"Well, I may not be a master of inhales, but I guarantee that Elohim wouldn't call you to more battles if He thought you couldn't handle them."

He reaches his hand over to mine and gives it a light squeeze before letting go. "Same dream last night?"

"A little different. I saw a new shadow walking toward me, and Elohim said to go. I have no idea where to, though."

Shea nods. "I thought maybe the dreams were pushing you toward something. Let's pray for Elohim to open a door." He stumbles to lift himself up.

I leap to my feet and offer him a hand.

Gripping me for support, Shea stands, then paces silently, a sign he's sharing his requests to Elohim.

I close my eyes and inhale. What can I learn about Elohim? He is kind, loving, slow to anger, good. My exhale is longer than it was before, and I release a quiet laugh. Elohim is my breath. When I recall who He is, surely He'll show me where to go.

After twenty minutes of prayer and silence, a bird flies overhead. As it comes closer, I recognize the giant wings and brown feathers as Faith. She lands on the grass near me, the flap of her wing pushing my hair back. She cries in a shrill whistle, then settles on the dirt.

Shea raises a brow and nudges his head in her direction.

I scurry toward Faith and stroke her feathers. "Good girl." She trills from my touch and low voice. Moving to the satchel attached to her back, I open the leather flap and remove three letters. Every month, Faith delivers one letter to Bahar and one to Alexis. Sure enough, two envelopes are addressed from Sam and to both Sam's mom and mine. I pause on the third.

"Who did Sam address the third one to?" Shea asks from behind me.

I clear my throat, my morning voice weak. Or perhaps it's from the way my heart skipped a beat without warning. "It's to me."

4

HIDE

PERO

The paper crinkles under the grip of my trembling hand. I loosen my hold. At the closing of Sam's letters to Mom and Alexis, he ended with "Say hi to my Ruth" or "How's Pero?", but he never wrote to me. Why talk to me now? And so bold too, with mentions of his past proposal and what I mean to him. I read again.

These storms disrupt my solitude, pushing me elsewhere. A new season. Perhaps that involves you. Oh, how I pray it does!

Sam would never lie, but his sincerity makes me pause. He wrote to me because Green Meadow calls for me. Not him. I'm a solution to his circumstance, nothing more. As a friend, he's asking for a favor, if I can even call us friends after five years without talking. He might have a girlfriend. Not that I care.

How should I respond? I could tell him I'm busy conquering cities, but that hasn't happened in a while. I could mention having to care for my parents...who are healthy and could manage fine without me. Or I could be honest and tell him I won't go because it's inconvenient, scary, and my Elohim-given powers won't restore a town, even if Elohim Himself told me to go in last night's dream. He hadn't specified where I should go, so what makes me assume this is my opportunity?

"There you are." Mom reaches the top of the hill near the tree where Shea left me alone about an hour earlier.

I fold the letter and shove it into my pocket.

"Is that from Sam?" She raises a brow. "I recognize the paper."

"Did you come for something specific?"

Mom gives me a funny look, then seems to let it go, as if she senses my inhibition.

I'm unsure why I won't show her. It's only a letter from a man I'm enamored with in my dreams. *Enamored? Wake-up-call, Pero. We're in reality, not an episode of* When Calls the Heart. I cross my arms and fidget to stop the blush creeping up my neck.

"Um, Shea's giving orders for us to pack up today."

"We arrived yesterday."

Below us, the Lesaries shake dust out of mats and fold down tents. We've settled several thousands of Lesaries in different cities along our journey. My family hasn't felt Elohim tell us to land in one place yet, so we keep moving. I hope wherever we end up is together and that Alexis, Cathena, Shea, Jehoshua, and Cherry are there. It's a lot to ask, I know.

"We're almost to the next city. Should be our last battle, and then we can settle more tribes."

"It won't be our last."

"How do you know?"

"Might not be public knowledge, but Shea said we have several more to come."

Mom sighs. "I shouldn't complain. Shea's had enough whining from Lesaries. I don't understand why so many consider returning to slavery better than fighting battles." She chuckles, then turns somber. "We are in the land Elohim promised, but I wonder when I'll finally have a home."

"I get it. It's not that I don't mind walking with the Lesaries. We're family, but it would be a lot easier to stay in one spot without Elohim calling me anywhere else."

"*Has* Elohim called you somewhere?" Mom glances at my pocket where the letter feels like fire burning a hole through fabric and into my skin.

But I don't want Sam's words to reach inside me and flow to my heart where there's room for my feelings to get all mixed up. I'd rather leave him at a safe distance so I can think. "Maybe He has."

"What makes you unsure?"

The truth trails across my mind, making my palms sweat and stomach lurch. "Elohim told me to go in a dream, and with Sam offering an opportunity, I should take it. I'm still having dreams about Sam, but I'm afraid to see him. I guess I'm nervous that if I go, I won't return to Origo. I can't leave you and Dad."

"Because of our separation in the past?"

"I think so."

"Does it also have something to do with Sam's proposal years ago?"

"Maybe."

Mom nods. "He invited me too."

I glance at Mom, hope rising in my breath. "He didn't mention that."

"My guess is he's leaving the decision up to you, no matter if I'm there or not."

"Are you going?"

A short pause, then Mom's response drenches in hesitation. "I don't know."

I wipe sweat from my forehead, my voice unsteady like it was the first time I asked her this question. Three-year-old me clung to Mom's leg, begging her to stay. Now, my gut says to go, and Mom doesn't plead for me to stick around. She'd let me leave without her if she knew it was my destiny, just as she left her little girl, because it would prove to be the right thing later. But oh, how painful were those years!

I step forward. "Don't let me leave you. I want to go or stay wherever you are. We both belong with the Lesaries and Elohim. If one of us were to be separated again, I couldn't handle it."

"Pero, we've been in Origo for a while. I question whether this invite applies to us both."

I twirl my hair into a tight curl around my finger. "What about the three chosen? Elohim has always used us three together."

"Not always. While you were still a baby, Elohim called me to start what you finished later with me and Sam. He prepared us three individually before He called us together. And the prophecy said we were chosen to bring Moon City's walls down. The next part of that prophecy didn't involve me."

"The lineage to the coming Messiah would continue through Sam and my marriage." I gulp. "What if the prophecy was wrong?"

"Don't you worry about that. If the prophecy is true, Elohim will make it clear. His ways bring peace, not confusion."

Peace seems like a distant mirage right now, perhaps because I'm thinking too much.

"I'll pray about if I should go with you." Mom's statement drips with finality, as if she had to say that in order to give more space to a decision she's already made. She isn't going. Which means I must grow up, charting my own course away from familiarity.

Is being an adult always this hard?

Mom and I startle when a figure appears out of thin air atop the hill where we're standing.

"Cathena!" I place a hand to my quick-beating heart. "Your transporting powers are creeping me out!"

Cathena's red hair shines vibrantly, bringing an ethereal glow to her pale face, but she doesn't laugh as usual after making a sudden appearance.

"Is something wrong?" Mom asks.

"It's Matthew," Cathena says.

I fight for breath. "Is he hurt?"

Cathena shakes her head. "Not exactly. Your dad collapsed and is—"

Mom hurries down the hill. With a lump caught in my throat, I follow, wondering if this might be my excuse to stay.

5

RUN

PERO

Dear Sam.

Using Mom's feather pen, I scratch out the formal greeting. I can start a letter better than that.

Hi there, buddy! What's kicking?

Too trendy. Another cross out.

What's new, you hot thing?

Seriously! What is wrong with me? I dig the pen into the paper and scribble over the words furiously, then I crumple it into a ball and toss the wad into the open fire. At least the flames are a good cover for the blush I sense on my face. Thankfully, the few people remaining outside are far away. I watch the dwindling flames in the pit nearest to my tent. The fire cooked our food hours ago, and most Lesaries retreated to their tents after evening stories and songs. Mom hasn't left Dad's side since he became ill three days ago.

A high fever, massive headaches, and nausea had doctors guessing it's a virus, but his symptoms haven't improved, which makes us wonder if there's something more serious. I can't leave to help Sam. It's more important that I support Mom with Dad's care. This is my answer. Am I using this as an excuse?

Maybe. But Sam will understand, if I can figure out how best to tell him.

Hot thing? I swear, my thoughts are creepy and completely unpredictable. I let out a nervous laugh, then grab the last piece of paper and breathe in.

Hi Sam,

I write out the greeting, tilting my head. Yes, that will work. Not too presumptuous, yet not too formal.

Great to hear from you. ~~Funny you should write to me since I've been dreaming about you for the last five years.~~ Alexis (Mom) gave me updates about how you're doing, but it's nice to hear directly from you. Not that I was upset you hadn't written to me. Really, I'm okay. More than okay. Life here is great. Except for my dad's health as of a few days ago. We're not sure what's going on, but he needs me right now. So does Mom. Which is why I am ~~incapable~~ unable to help you and Green Meadow. But I am sorry to hear about the situation.

I heard Green Meadow was going through unusual storms, but I hadn't heard it became that bad. We've had continuous heat waves. Everything is dry here, which feels like a curse of some sort, but no storms. Are you sure you should stay? It seems like it would be a lot safer if you took Carper's offer and got on the next plane to China. Honestly, it scares me to go to a place that everyone else is running away from. I feel like I've had enough adventures. Though, I tend to be on the cautious side, or maybe my dad's anxiety is getting to me. He's not anxious like he used to be, mostly because Mom (Bahar) and he are finally together again. Still, if my dad could tell me what he thought about me going, I think he would suggest I stay. I realize as an adult, I can make my own choices, but based on your descriptions of a town I used to love, I think the best option is for you to leave. I'm concerned that you're following a dream that will kill you if you're not careful. Be safe, please. Bahar and Alexis can't bear to lose one of their children again.

About your letter. I had no idea you could be so poetic. So renaissance romantic. I like it. I guess I shouldn't be surprised when you have a mysterious depth about you, like there are layers of insight in your core that you intentionally expose at the right moment. How do you do that?

I'm going to be honest with you, Sam, and try my hardest not to cross out what I say next, especially when I'm on the other side of my last piece of paper and this letter is getting longer by the minute. I was young when we first met. Only seventeen. Looking back, I wonder how much of our "connection" was from me being easily infatuated with any guy who looked my way, but also partly because we were the chosen. Regardless of what I felt between us then, I'm sorry for breaking your heart.

Over the last few years, I'm grateful for everything Elohim has become to me without a boyfriend. I've cherished these last five years spent with Him and the Lesarien family. As awkward and anxious as I can be, I've matured, and I'm thankful that Elohim brings me to uncomfortable places in order to grow. Except for when I refuse to go. Still working on that maturity thing.

The more I think about it, the more I realize that your depth could be what has kept you in Green Meadow when everyone else was leaving. You mentioned the door hasn't opened for you to enter this universe, but you could've at least left the storm. You didn't. You have such conviction to hold fast to the place Elohim has planted you, even if what you've planted in your garden hasn't taken root. I admire you for staying true to your calling.

See? I can sound poetic too. :)

I should cross out everything I said before and start this letter again. It's sort of become a diary.

Okay, here's the deal. Before I give the final "no" to coming like I already did at the beginning of this letter, let me pray about it like I should've in the first place. If I do go, I may bring Cathena. Mom's unsure if she's supposed to go, and Cathena's become a mighty warrior for Elohim thanks to Carper's superb training back in the Moon City days when Cathena's name was Stone. Carper may not deserve that kind of credit when he originally intended it for evil, yet I'm grateful for the friend Cathena has become to me and my parents. Side note, you wouldn't believe the way her red hair has darkened, or has it brightened? It's electrifying, like a crosswalk vest, and completely natural. So unfair.

I'll pray for your protection, Sam. Hang in there. Or leave if it's safer, unless I change my mind and come to help you. Then you should stay because I'd hate to arrive in a storm alone, or just me and a fire-hair-girl. (Cathena scares me way too often. If I were a cat, I'd have three lives left, so maybe I shouldn't bring her along. If you ever see her again in person, you'll get what I mean.)

I remain your awkward Pero. (I'd sign with Ruth, but I'm sure a Ruth would never embarrass herself so severely. Don't you think Ruth is a refined name? While I'm writing my next letter, I'll sip peppermint tea and pet wild roadrunners. Only then will I consider myself Ruth-worthy.)

Your friend,
Pero

P.S. You can call me Ruth if you'd like. It goes well with

your whole poetic vibe. ;) Can I call you by your middle name, Boaz? Or how about Bo? Nah. You are a Sam to me and Salmon to our moms.

Goodnight, sweet Sam.

P.P.S. Write to me again, and tell me you're safe. I'm sure Alexis mentioned that I have no boyfriend to get jealous over letters sent from a man. Then again, you may have a wife now, and if so, don't write to me.

WITH LITTLE INK REMAINING, I scribble over the sentences I'd be mortified for Sam to see. Folding the letter, I find Faith at the edge of a cluster of trees and burrowing her head into her feathers, fast asleep. I approach the harness on her back and gently place the letter in the leather pocket. An ordinary eagle would scream at me, peck my eyes with its beak, and scratch me with its killer claws. But Faith is far from ordinary.

"You have a softer pillow than I do," I whisper, then place my hand on her back. "Lucky ducky."

Faith opens her eyes, her wings tightening before relaxing under my touch. She closes her eyes again, drifting to sleep.

"Sorry for calling you a duck. How many lives do enormous eagles have, anyway? You seem like the type to live forever." My empty fist tightens. "I bet you're not afraid."

After a few strokes on her neck, I say goodnight, leave her purring, and stumble in the dark to find my own peaceful sleep.

6

———————

FIND

SAM

Dear Ruth,

I received your letter. Don't worry about me. Elohim protects those He chooses to carry out His plan.

Thank you for praying about the matter. I'd never pressure you into coming. I'm happy that you responded. I wondered if…. Well, no worries.

Thank you, too, for your honesty. Vulnerability is a rare gift, and I like you all the more for it. I'm sorry to hear about your dad. That's so difficult, and I understand your commitment to stay in Origo and help him. Give Mom (Bahar) a big hug for me, and tell her if there's anything she needs Faith to deliver—medicine, herbs, etc—let me know. Somehow, Faith still has access through the portal in the sky. But I do not. I found out the hard way when Faith flew through a cloud, and I fell off of her. I was prepared with a parachute. One can never be too careful.

I'm including a whole stack of paper and a pen with this letter so you have enough space to remove whatever you're not ready to share. But even if you don't edit, your words will bring a smile to my face. You make me laugh. In a good way.

I don't mind what you call me. I knew a Bo once. He was a nice and highly educated engineer, the complete opposite of a Sam. But a profession or culture doesn't always match the meaning of a name. My full name, Salmon, means peace, and Boaz means strength. I'll let you decide if either of those is true of me.

While I'm sure the wild roadrunners wouldn't mind you petting them as you're sipping mint tea, refinement doesn't describe you. At least, not from my perspective. The true meaning of your middle name is friend and a vision of beauty. I whole-heartedly agree.

Your Humble Poet,
Sam

P.S. No, I'm not married.

7

CHOOSE

SAM

Faith arrives in front of The Daily Grind, the next store on my rotation of break-ins. If I steal food from a different place each trip, maybe it won't hurt Green Meadow's economy as badly. At least, I hope embezzling supplies won't cause too much trouble when people return. Drones with cameras and the words *OBC News* follow me, but Monica didn't offer free food delivery when she interviewed me. OBC seeks a successful story and my survival.

With a hammer and blanket in hand, I leap from Faith's back, proceeding to the sliding glass doors. A quick punch through the glass gives me a way in.

"Wait a minute." I give the command for Faith to stay.

She sits.

I step through the entrance. When no alarm sounds, I unlock the door. A switch on a nearby panel sets it automatically open, leaving enough room for Faith to enter. I lay the blanket over the shards of glass. Nudging my head in my eagle's direction, I give a low whistle. "Careful, now."

She trots inside, her beak shifting back and forth to check everything out before taking more steps forward.

"Alright." I pop my knuckles, then grab a cart. "Now for the fun stuff."

Down aisle four, I balance a can of beans in the palm of my hand, holding it up toward Faith. "Do beans taste okay without a microwave?"

She cocks her head as if pondering and pecks it from my hand. The can falls on the linoleum floor, denting its top.

"You spilled the beans." I smile, then pick the can up and put it into the cart. "Should I feel guilty stealing food from a deserted grocery store?"

Faith trots down the aisle, no doubt in search of saltine crackers.

"You're walking away from confrontation again."

She scours the bags of popcorn kernels, tearing at the plastic.

"I promise I'll pay the store back whenever it opens and replace the window I broke to get in here."

Kernels explode down the aisle as the bag rips open.

"That's one way to pop the corn." Pushing the cart down the aisle, I call out to my unusually large eagle. "You're responsible for your own mess."

I leave Faith to play tug-of-war with the grains while I search for peanut butter and question my sanity. I'm talking to an animal. Can I live alone in a deserted town for much longer? I don't talk to my tacos, so I should be good. How did the first man manage to survive without a grocery store?

I've been thinking about Adam lately. Partly because I'm alone, but also because I can't help connecting Adam's situation with my own. Elohim formed Adam from dirt, and although He breathed life into the first man's form, Adam's heart hardened, similar to the dirt I try to cultivate on my property. It was alive, but now it's completely hard.

As Adam longed for Eve, I wish for a partner, specifically someone who also has a gift to grow things. Not literally, like I can, but I haven't met any other whose song softens the hardest of hearts. Pero is the one to break Green Meadow's curse. Pero is my Eve.

Last night, I dreamt that I owned and operated a field of grain. Harvesters worked in my field, and I paid them at the end of their day.

"Elohim be with you," I said to the workers. "Koach to you."

"And to you," they said.

I distinctly heard one familiar voice above the others and searched for her until she came into view.

Ruth appeared older, yet more beautiful than ever. Dark hair cascaded over one shoulder and enhanced brown eyes, her skin the same color as the stalks of wheat in a basket balanced on her curved hip. Her posture exuded grace and charm, and her smile brightened enough to blind me.

Faith trots around the corner. A plastic bag around her foot makes a soft cracking sound with every step. She joins me in front of the variety of peanut butter.

"Crunchy or creamy?" With no response from Faith, I sigh. "If only you were Balam's donkey and could talk."

Faith stomps her foot to remove the plastic.

"Come here, girl." I bend down and remove the bag. Crinkling it in my hand, another sigh escapes from deeper in my core. "What if she refuses to come? If it doesn't work out, it isn't meant to be. But these dreams." *Elohim, remove my thoughts of her away if they have no purpose. Better yet, bring my Eve to me.*

A crash comes from the freezer section two aisles over. "What was that?"

I pause and listen. So does Faith. When nothing happens, I pick up a jar of crunchy peanut butter and throw it into the cart. "Probably a display that fell."

At the aisle's end, I stop suddenly and step back. A mirage of someone stands in front of me. No, it's real. The figure takes the shape of a young woman with fiery red hair, an hour-glass contour, and sharp gray eyes. She wears a leather jacket and skinny jeans. Her features are exotic, almost too beautiful to look at, so I glance away. She's not Pero.

I blink, then open my eyes to see her standing in front of me. As real as my racing pulse.

"You must be Sam." Her voice is as melodic as a soprano opera singer. "My name is Cathena."

"I've heard you tend to appear out of nowhere."

Her brows lift. "Did I scare you?"

"A little."

"Good. I scare Pero most often."

Faith comes around the corner and approaches Cathena.

"Your eagle isn't afraid of anyone." She reaches a hand out to pet Faith. "Maybe she remembers me from the occasional visits to Origo."

Getting straight to the point, I ignore the casual observations. "Why are you here? Pero mentioned you're a transporter, but I didn't expect you to land in Green Meadow."

"Me neither. My assignments are unpredictable. Did you recently pray for Elohim to bring you someone?"

"Yes, but you weren't the person I was thinking of. No offense."

Cathena nods. "I would've dragged Pero with me if I had control over the matter."

"In her last letter, Pero said she'd bring you with her if she were to come."

"And I'm still willing once she makes her choice, but I'm here for a different reason. Occasionally, Elohim gives me messages for others. Usually, I show up to rescue someone. Like when I appeared in Beijing to help Pero escape."

"Which one is it now?" I don't think it's the best idea for me to leave, but if Elohim wants it, I will.

"A message."

I release a held breath. As dangerous as Green Meadow has become, I'm not ready to leave.

"It doesn't make sense to me, but Elohim's words seldom do."

I raise a brow, waiting for her to continue.

"Trust nature."

"That's it?"

Cathena holds her hands up. "Like I said, I have no idea. I'm only the messenger, and the message seems clear in here." She points to her head.

I scratch my neck, then fold my arms. "Hmm." I trust Elohim and His plan for me to stay. I trust He will provide a way for the storms to settle. But to trust the storm itself seems a stretch. Isn't nature against me? "Thank you, Cathena. I'll think about what you said."

She gives a curt nod. "You're welcome." An awkward silence follows. "I'll let you return to your shopping."

"That's it?"

"I'm unsure what else I'm here for. If there isn't another reason, I expect to disappear any second now." She looks at her wrist-watch and taps her foot. "Can I help you shop while I'm waiting?" She sweeps the premises. "You weren't kidding when you told your moms it was empty around here."

I don't say anything. Maybe I'm shocked that she appeared out of thin air and isn't sure what's next. Does Elohim intend to bring me Cathena instead of Pero? I never dream of a red-haired girl. Then again, I can't help but notice her exotic charm.

Cathena examines my cart. "Crunchy peanut butter? How could you even consider such a texture?"

"Oh, uh—"

"Creamy with Oreos is the way to go, at least for me and Pero."

"I didn't know."

Cathena gives a sideways grin. "You don't get me. No prob.

Takes weeks, which we may not have." She glances at her watch again. "How are you coping with the storms?"

"I get to enjoy breaks every once in a while." I pause. "I'm not stealing, in case you were wondering."

"I wasn't."

"I keep track of everything so I can pay the store back."

"Do you think anyone will return?"

I shrug. "Hope so."

"Cool." She sniffs, then tugs at her leather jacket nervously. "How's Matthew?"

"Not any better. Bahar and Pero are taking good care of him though."

"I have no doubt." We turn down another aisle. "And Pero?"

"What about her?" Cathena asks.

"How is she?"

"She's all right."

"Like in a bad way?"

"No, in a good way. She's good."

"Good." I scratch my head. "Anything else?"

"Nope."

"I guess you'll be sticking around then, which is okay with me. Want any other food while we're here? I'm cooking canned beans for dinner, so now's your chance."

"Beans are fine. Thanks." She pauses. "Actually, if you don't mind, I'd like some Oreos."

"Aisle three has leftover yellow ones from Easter."

Cathena grins. "Sounds dee-lish. I'll be back."

"You won't disappear?"

"Can't guarantee."

Two minutes later, she returns with double-stuffed Oreos, and Faith flies us to the farm.

Imagine a twenty-five-year-old man who lives alone. (Think hermit on Walden's Pond.) Let's say that this twenty-five-year-old man wishes for a pretty wife. (I know who first comes to mind, but Taylor Swift's not his type.) One day, a gorgeous and kind woman suddenly appears to this said hermit's home and eats a can of beans and Oreos with *creamy* peanut butter at his kitchen table. (He can't explain what compelled him to leave the crunchy behind while she was on aisle three.)

Is this woman an answer to this man's prayer? Happenstance? A cheap date with no further implications?

She's still in my house, at my kitchen table, scooping up large amounts of creamy goodness onto her cookie and chewing slowly before swallowing. I'm sure sugar is a welcoming treat when she's spent recent years in Origo with the Lesaries. All those wild roadrunners Pero's been playing with can't be too satisfying.

Cathena brought me a message from Elohim, but Elohim hadn't sent her away. Why is she still here? She isn't the girl of my dreams. Perhaps she's supposed to be. My heart skips a beat for a moment. Didn't Pero mention before that Cathena and Henry were an item?

I clear my throat. "Any word from Henry?" That was casual, right? She has to recall Henry and I were best friends for a while.

After chewing and swallowing, she clears her throat with a glass of water. "He's fine."

Not exactly an answer to my question. Should I probe deeper? I decide against it. If she wants to tell me more, she will.

"This dessert is better than I remember," she says. "You shouldn't have replaced the peanut butter for me, though."

"It's not a problem. I like both options."

"So does Pero." She picks at her bowl of beans with her spoon. "You and Henry were close friends for a while. He mentioned you often, but he never did contact you. It's none of my business, of course, but I am curious if there was a disagreement between you two."

If I knew she'd include Henry and Pero in the same thought, I wouldn't have brought up his name. Our shared interest was one girl. It seems silly now. We were two competitive boys craving the attention of Bahar's mysterious daughter.

"Never mind that," Cathena says. "You don't have to share."

"No." I extend my hand. "It's okay. We...uh...we shared affections for the same girl."

Her eyes brighten as if she understands who I refer to. "I see."

"We were still friends. No hard feelings. But shortly after that, Henry stayed in China and I landed here. We naturally drifted apart."

Her face darkens. "I wish he'd told me. I would have understood." She fidgets in her seat. "Henry and I are taking a break. It wouldn't be fair for me to explain why." Standing to her feet, Cathena picks up her bowl and spoon and takes them to the sink. The hole in the wall above the sink serves as a very large window. Cathena doesn't seem to be bothered by it. Maybe she would be if there was an actual storm outside. Come to think of it, why isn't it raining?

"Thank you for the...um, the dinner."

I stand up and approach the sink. "Don't worry about the dishes. The water isn't running, so I have my own system for cleaning with jugs." Or I stick the plates through the hole in the wall one by one, let the rain wash them clean. But she doesn't need to know I'm that resourceful.

"Okay, well, thanks again for letting me be here and giving up your room." She slowly backs up until bumping into the corner of the counter. "I'll be heading to bed, then. Unless you'll let me swap with you. I'm used to sleeping in a tent on hard ground. I don't mind the couch."

"You might as well enjoy a comfortable mattress while staying here."

She nods. "Goodnight."

"Goodnight." I avert my eyes to her retreating form. Good grief. What is wrong with me? As if I've never seen an attractive woman. But this close and in my house, sleeping in my bed. I shake my head, suddenly noticing my lack of fresh air.

"Sam?" Cathena swivels on her heel to look at me.

"Yeah?" My voice sounds weak. *I'm* weak!

"You're a good man."

Am I?

She tilts her head. "I don't understand why Elohim hasn't transported me to Origo, but I'm not the one you've been waiting for."

I feel warmth trail up my neck. Has my curiosity been that obvious?

"And for what it's worth, I think Pero likes you."

I swallow hard. "What makes you think that?"

"Her hesitation to accept your invitation. She feels anxious when she wants to be close to someone but is unsure how to be."

Sounds like Pero. "Are there more reasons you've come to that conclusion?"

"Yeah. Every night, you're in her dreams."

I grip the refrigerator handle. I'm in *Ruth's* dreams; she's in mine. This can't be a coincidence. And here I am mixing up my passions over a pretty woman. Cathena isn't a part of my past and barely in my present. Only one has been a critical part of both, and I still desperately long for her in my future.

"Goodnight, Cathena." I smile, then head toward the front door to get that much needed night air.

8

MOVE

SAM

The early light wakes me from too few hours of sleep. I rub my eyes, then roll to my side on the couch. Last night, I wandered the gardens until far past midnight. It was the clearest night I'd seen in a while, but between Sleeping Beauty in my bed and Pero on my mind, I couldn't sleep. Cathena's right about her not being the one for me. So why is she still here?

With a stretch and yawn, I get up and drag my feet to the kitchen, where I pour a cup of cold-brew. A bird lands on the ledge of the hole above my kitchen sink, the first creature I've seen besides Faith in a long while. I tip my mug toward the robin.

"Good morning, neighbor."

It shakes in response, showing off a mass of wet, fluffy feathers.

I lean my head through the hole, and the bird takes off. "No rain this morning." I tuck my head back inside and bring the mug to my lips. *Strange.* Usually the storm doesn't stop for two days in a row.

A little red blinking light on the Keurig catches my attention. The microwave also winks with neon green digital numbers. My eyes widen. "Electricity!"

How? Does it matter? Would rather not waste my thoughts wondering.

Dumping out my mug of poor-man's liquid, I snatch a pod from the cupboard and stuff it into the machine. I'm about to pour the water from a store-bought jug, then decide to check the faucet. It's working! With a laugh and a little dance, I make my cup of hot coffee. What next? Shower or breakfast? I'm tempted to take a lengthy shower after months of succumbing to bathing in bone-chilling flood waters from the creek nearby. But the electricity could cut out again at any minute, unless Cathena *is* the reason the storms stopped and things are returning to normal. Let's not get ahead of things. It's only electricity. And calm weather.

I scan the cupboard for anything I could cook on the stove and find a box of unopened pancake mix. "Perfect." I throw together an eggless batter and heat the stovetop to warm a cast iron pan.

After the pan warms up, I pour the batter and watch it sizzle. A sweet and buttery smell fills the air. I'll never take a pancake for granted again. From my bedroom, Cathena stirs. Great timing. I'll have a robust breakfast in fifteen minutes, the least I can offer after last night's meager meal. I'm on my second cake when the phone rings, making me jump. The first call I've had since yesterday's interview, and before that... I don't remember. Perhaps months prior. My phone's charged, and service is back. This is good. Maybe I won't need Pero after all. I cringe. If everything gets better, will I still want her?

The number on the screen is unknown. I pick up the phone and answer. "Hello?"

"Sam? Can you hear me?"

"Yes. Can you hear me? Who is this?"

"This is Steven Wayne. I'm the weather anchor for the Oregon Broadcasting Company."

"Of course. I know who you are." A tremor passes through me. Not because of Steven, but the impact if everyone knew the power's back on. In their excitement, people will surge into Green Meadow, and I'm not ready for chaos. Not to mention the paparazzi who could surround my home or climb in it. I'm missing a sizable chunk of my kitchen, for goodness' sake!

"Wonderful, Steven says. "We received word from the American Drone Safety Services that electricity and cell service have been restored. Anything new happen that would cause this positive change?"

"I'm unsure if this has anything to do with it, but a woman showed up last night and is at my house now."

Steven chuckles. "That's not the kind of positive change or service I was referring to."

"What?" My face flushes when I realize my awkward answer. "No, sir. It's not like that. I just met her and…"

Steven's robust laughter makes it clear my explanation isn't working.

A voice sounds from behind me. "Is everything okay?"

I spring, then swivel, spatula in hand and aimed toward Cathena, who's dressed in one of my shirts and her jeans from yesterday. "You startled me." I safely lower my spatula and return to the phone. "Not you, Steven. Cathena's here—"

"Who's Cathena?" he asks.

"Sam, the stove!" Cathena points.

Smoke is billowing from the pan. "Shoot." The phone clatters to the countertop. I remove the cake, turn off the burner, and start the overhead fan. Remembering the breezy hole in the wall, I stop the fan. When I touch the skillet's iron handle, my hand throbs. "Ouch." I turn on the faucet and let my fingers cool under the water.

"Are you still there?" I hear Steven yell through the phone.

I pick it up. "Here."

"Are you hurt?"

"No. Only a minor burn. Guess it's been too long since I tried to multi-task."

Another chuckle. "I'll tell you what. While our luck is hot, I'm gonna swing over to your place with my crew. Wouldn't want to miss a pivotal moment."

I turn off the water and weave around Cathena, who's traded spots with me at the stove and is finishing making breakfast.

I mouth, *thank you.*

A questioning look plays on her face, but she remains silent.

"With all due respect, Steven, it's a little soon to risk a trip here. Things changed only moments ago. We don't know yet how everything will pan out."

Cathena smirks and points to the skillet. "No pun intended?"

Steven's raised voice interrupts my laugh at Cathena's quick catch.

"You've got to be kidding!"

I turn down the volume.

"Sam, this is the story of a century! When the world finds out you predicted the future, you'll be a sensation. It's a new beginning for Green Meadow."

"Uh...what do you mean I 'predicted the future'?"

"The last interview with Monica?"

I try to focus on what he could be talking about, but come up with nothing.

"Monica asked how you knew you would survive, and you said the solution to stopping the storms was—"

I gasp. "A woman?"

"Your words, Sam."

"Hold on. You think the storm stopped because of

Cathena?" This isn't good.

Cathena glances my way, confusion on her face.

"Who's Cathena again?" Steven asks.

"The woman at my house right now."

"I thought you said a woman named Ruth would stop the storms."

I suppress a groan. It was a mistake to say so much in the interview. "Yes, those were my words."

"So, if I'm understanding correctly, your *Ruth* is a *Cathena*?"

"Now, I wouldn't assume...that is, I'm not sure if...."

Steven's laughter roars loud enough to shake the rest of the kitchen wall down. When he still hasn't calmed down after a moment, I nearly hang up.

He pauses. "I'm sorry, but, out of all the stories, this is the most remarkable piece I've ever.... People shadow me every-where, Sam. They stop me while I'm in the elevator, the hall-ways, even the *bathroom*, to pitch what they call the next big hit for the latest news. We're talkin' stories about toddlers saving cats and racoons entering town hall for Bingo night. Then you come along.... Okay, okay. Picture this: 'Twenty-four-year-old single man saves Green Meadow through his infatuation with beautiful women.' Can't you see it? We're rising to the top, man!"

His use of *we* doesn't slide past me. This is all a big joke to feed Steven's social status, but nothing I explain will make him believe me. I myself am not sure what to believe. "Not inter-ested. Please, don't come to my home."

"My chopper will land in your yard. See you soon, Sam."

I don't reply, my broiling blood summoning enough fury to become another storm or incinerate the next flippin' pancake.

Silence follows as he ends the call.

"Breakfast is ready," Cathena says.

"Kay." Sitting at the dining room table, I cradle my head in my hands, then feel a steady throb from the skillet's burn and set them down.

"What was that call about?"

"A news reporter is coming by helicopter today. Wants to interview me about my so-called infatuation with women."

"I don't understand." Cathena frowns.

"I made a comment during the last interview about the third chosen being the one to stop the storms."

"You didn't!" She sets a stack of unburnt pancakes and syrup on the table, followed by plates and forks, then sits down next to me.

"I'm afraid, I did." I sigh, then pick up my fork and dig into my first bite. "Thanks for saving the food."

"You're welcome."

My shirt hangs loose on Cathena's slight form. I turn my gaze. "You might consider changing into your clothes from yesterday if Steven comes. It wouldn't help my reputation with you wearing that."

"Understood."

We eat in silence for a moment.

Cathena leaves the table and returns with two mugs of hot coffee, as natural as if she's been helping in my house for years.

I stare at the steam rising. "This doesn't feel right."

"It's a better alternative than the instant, kinda-cold brew you've been drinking."

I shake my head. "That's not what I mean. You, me, in my house. You in my clothes. It feels too...."

"Intimate?"

"Something like that." I turn toward her. "The thing is, my parents had a similar thing happen when they first met, and by the end of the evening, my father proposed to my mom. Not that I'm planning the same."

Cathena takes a sip of her coffee before setting it down. "I'll leave."

How can she seem so calm when I'm not? Usually I'm the relaxed one.

"Where? You haven't been transported back home to Origo, so obviously you're supposed to be here."

Cathena grins. "If you haven't noticed, this town is pretty empty. There are plenty of houses or hotels to stay at."

"They may not be vacant. I'd hate for something to happen to you."

"Do you prefer I stay with you?"

I blink. "I expected Pero to come. Then you appear by yourself, and the storms stop, and the electricity is back. Maybe Steven's right. You being here has to mean something."

"Care to hear what I think?" She folds her fingers together and rests her chin against them, looking far more sweet than she should.

"Go for it."

"I think me staying here is a test for you to see how much you care for Pero."

If it's a test, I've already failed the second Cathena set foot in my house.

"How often have you thought about Pero in the last few months?" she asks.

I raise a brow. "Honestly? She's in my dreams every night."

"When she took off to find Henry in China—and yes, I'm aware about Pero and Henry—how did you feel?"

"Lonely, but that was a while ago."

"How long?" Cathena asks with a challenge in her tone.

"Almost a year."

"Right. And it's been five years for Pero in the other universe. Pero and I are both twenty-two, while you've remained about the same age."

I nod, uncertain where she's going with all of this.

"Have you ever been in love with Pero?"

"Yes." No hesitation.

"There you go." She reclines against her chair and crosses her arms, as if that one statement resolved all the world's problems. "This doesn't feel right because it's not. Don't let me get in the way of Elohim's plans." She stands. "Now, if you'll excuse me, I have a hotel to find. I'll check in with you tomorrow, if I'm still on Earth."

Thoughts swirl in my head like fireflies. "Yeah, sounds good." I give a wave, and she leaves me zoning out, praying that she's right, knowing that she has to be. I'm in love. Perhaps always have been.

An hour later, Steven Wayne's helicopter interrupts me from the same spot. I clear my throat and walk out the front door to watch him land on the large gravel driveway.

After he steps out of the chopper, I approach him. He extends his hand, and I shake it, cringing when the burn reminds me of its presence.

"Where's the girl?" He looks around with a huge grin on his face, as if I'm the joke of the day.

"She left."

The rest of the crew step out of the helicopter with their cameras and equipment.

"Where'd she go?"

"I'm not telling you where." I clamp my mouth shut.

Steven mumbles under his breath, then shouts louder than he did through the phone. "You'll find her and bring her here!"

"I'll do no such thing. She's not the one to calm the storm."

Steven laughs, which in person is far more obnoxious. "Have you looked around? The storms are gone. Not a cloud in the sky. The sun's out. I *will* feature this story."

I step closer. "You have five minutes to climb into your fancy contraption and get off my property."

He smiles knowingly yet obeys, turning toward the chopper. The crew follows. With a firm grip on the handle, he's about to step up when a rumble—deeper than the helicopter's rotors—shakes the ground.

I strain to listen and recognize the sharp cracking sound.

Steven looks around him with mouth hanging open, appearing unsure whether or not he should believe the earth is moving.

The sky turns gray, darkening by the second. A raindrop splashes on my head.

Steven takes one last look at me, then toward the ominous clouds. "Let's be going."

When he and his crew are out of sight, lightning crashes.

I shout above the wind that's picked up speed and give a shrill whistle with my fingers between my teeth. Faith flies toward me and lands. "It's going to be a big one." I hop onto her back. "Let's go find Cathena."

Faith soars at full speed as sheets of rain slap against us. "I can't see, Faith. We'll never find her like this."

I steer Faith toward the barn near my house and pray that Elohim transports Cathena back to Origo. A tree branch appears in front of me. Before I can pull away, it slams against my head, and the world turns dark.

9

———————

GO

PERO

Dad's eyes flutter open, and I move closer to him on the floor of the tent. Reaching for the cup of water nearby, I bring it toward his lips. "Drink some of this."

He lifts his head to take a few sips, then lays down.

"How are you feeling?" I rest my palm against his forehead. "Temperature seems better."

He clears his throat, then moves his lips, but no sound comes out.

"You don't have to speak. You're still recovering."

"How long have I...?" Dad wheezes.

"Been sick?"

He nods, then winces, the motion too strenuous.

"Four days."

Dad opens his eyes in alarm. "The Lesaries...."

"...are fine. Some have moved on to settle their tribes in new territories. The others can wait. Your health is more important."

His voice grows stronger, and he places a hand over my own. "Why are you here?"

"Really, Dad? It's the least I can do after everything you've done for me over the years. The doctors haven't figured out what's going on with you. Someone mentioned a virus, but if that were the case, I'd think others would have it. They tried all kinds of herbal teas and oils. I wish we were in the U.S. and could run tests."

"Pero." Dad chuckles softly. "I like it here."

"Me too," I mumble, then meet his face, full of curiosity. "I'm leaving tonight."

"Joining a different tribe?"

I shake my head. "Nothing like that." I pause, searching inside for the courage to voice the right words. Cathena disappeared several days ago, and although it could've been to China to visit Henry, that seems highly unlikely since their relationship is on pause. Sam is the only other person I could think to whom Elohim would send her. Perhaps it's because I denied the call to go. The truth is, I'd rather not have Cathena help Sam. She doesn't know him like I do. What if after one look at Cathena, Sam falls in love with her? With her gorgeous hair and self-confidence, any young man would be a fool to not look her way. My body tenses thinking of the possibility.

"I'm going to Earth. I'll look for medical supplies while I'm there. Maybe I can find a doctor. But don't worry. Mom is staying to take care of you."

Dad studies me. "You're going for more than one reason, aren't you?"

I nod. "Sam asked for my help."

A hint of a smile crosses his lips. "Did you finally say yes to his proposal?"

"What? No!" I hide my face with my hands.

His laughter brings hope that his health is improving. "I'm glad you're going."

"You are?"

"Well, yeah. You shouldn't be hanging around your sick old man. Besides, I'm feeling better already."

"Promise you'll keep getting better."

"I'll try my best." Dad closes his eyes to rest again.

I squeeze his hand, stand, and stretch. Mom and I rotate shifts, checking on him, giving him tinctures at every waking moment. But without modern medicine, I'm unsure if this unconventional method is enough to see him bounce back. What if he gets worse while I'm gone? My palms sweat. No, I can't think that way. Surely Elohim will heal him.

Stepping outside the tent, I take in the warm afternoon sun and Lesaries scattered about. Their eyes lock on mine—are those scowls on their faces? Some lounge in the shade; others stroll in circles like caged animals. A group of children sit in the dirt, playing a game with marbles and sticks. A woman about Dad's age named Brenda sees me and frowns.

"Is he finally ready?" Brenda calls while crossing her arms. "In all honesty, waiting around for one person is getting tiresome."

I never have cared for the lady. She looks for complaints and isn't afraid to voice them any chance she gets.

"Why didn't you join Asher when he left a few days ago?"

Brenda crosses her arms. "I'm not leaving Shea's tribe."

I shrug, then purse my lips before anything comes out of my mouth that shouldn't. It's not Dad's fault that he's sick. Lesaries have stuck together for over forty years. Can't they survive a few days longer?

"He's feeling a lot better today, Brenda. Thanks for caring so much." I walk away, the anger starting to dwindle.

When I enter my own tent, I finish making preparations for my trip to Earth. I don't own much to put into Jimmy's old bag: hair brush, toothpaste, one change of clothes, my feather necklace. I reach into the bag and pull out the necklace. It's been a while since I've worn it. The string tying it together has shriveled, held together by meager threads. I remove the pendant off the string and give it a squeeze. I need all the *koach* I can get on this trip, and the feather accompanied me through many trials and joys: falling in love, finding my bio parents, reuniting with Mom and Dad, coming to faith in Elohim. I place the pendant gently in my pocket. Funny how a small trinket can be the ideal companion.

"Knock, knock." A voice sounds through the tent's entrance. "It's me."

"Come in, Mom."

She opens the flap, then ducks in. "Your bag's more brown than green now."

I finger the scratchy surface. "If you look closely, you can still see traces of Jimmy's blood. Makes me sad when I think about it."

"Then why carry it?"

"Feels like I'm honoring a past friend, I guess."

Mom sits on the ground next to me. "You're still sure about going without me?"

"Yeah." I pinch my shoulder blades as if sitting up taller will bring more certainty. "Dad stayed awake to chat with me."

"Great! In a couple of days, I'm sure he'll be on his feet."

"I told him I was going," I say. "He asked if I finally said yes to one of Sam's proposals."

Mom laughs. "What'd you tell him?"

Is she seriously asking me this question? "I said no."

"Don't be too quick to dismiss the idea, Pero."

"The idea of what? Sam hasn't proposed again." Not that I expect him to. "He might not be interested in me any more."

A knowing gleam rests in her eyes.

"He said something about me in one of his letters, didn't he?"

"It's up to you to find out."

I groan. "What if I don't like him in that way? Did you ever consider that possibility?"

"I don't believe it for a second."

"Well, believe it. I'm not interested in starting a relationship with Sam Nesim."

"You mean those dreams you've had of him for *five* years haven't meant anything?"

I look down to hide the blush I feel on my face. Might as well tell her the truth. She reads me too well to hide secrets. "Okay, maybe I like him a little."

Mom wraps her arm around my shoulder. "Elohim..."

I close my eyes when I realize she's praying.

"...protect Pero. Calm the storms in Green Meadow and in her heart. Cause her to recognize where you'll lead her. Amen."

I open my eyes and give Mom a squeeze. She's good at immediately directing her worries to Elohim. "Thanks, Mom. Take care of Dad for me."

"You bet I will." She kisses my head. "Have you said goodbye to your other mom yet?"

"Alexis is next on my list."

"Perfect. You're one lucky girl to have so many parents who love you."

I rest my head against hers. "That's what makes it hard to leave."

"We're still your biggest fans, but it's challenging to let you go, especially as a mother."

I am like a bird being pushed out of the nest when the mother senses she's ready to fly.

"I can do this," I say. And for a moment, I believe it.

10

ARRIVE

PERO

Alexis is beside me when we approach a large tree.

"Seems like this would be the one." When placing a hand on the trunk, nothing warms beneath my touch. No light, no emerging walkways. Nothing but rough bark. I was so focused on deciding to go to Earth I forgot I could use an opening.

"Maybe there's another way?" Alexis runs a hand through her hair.

"I expected a door in this tree. It's the only one around here big enough for me to fit through."

"Perhaps there's no opening because of Green Meadow's curse."

"What do you mean?" I ask.

"Well, if you think about it, Sam's gardening gift isn't working, so he currently doesn't have the ability to make doors open."

"Can't Elohim make it happen, though?"

Alexis nods. "For sure, but He also uses Sam's gift of growing things to demonstrate His power."

Setting myself down at the base of the tree, I lean back.

"Well then, I guess I'll be sitting here until something happens."

Alexis joins me, and we stay this way for a moment.

"What if I'm not supposed to go?" Maybe no door means no-can-do.

"Sam needs you."

"Of course you'd say that. You raised him, so you know him best. But me?" Moving a hand on my chest, I leave it resting against my heart. "What's my next step when I get there? Sing to the rain? Ask him to marry me and the storm will stop? I'm not the one for this."

"Pero, I understand you better than I'm given credit for. You like him. It's been written all over your face whenever I've told you about his letters."

I smile and look the other way. "What if Elohim's best is me being the solution to a single man's problems?" I grimace. "That sounded wrong."

Alexis chuckles. "From my perspective, I'd say you're *living* Elohim's best for you. I don't see you rushing into or away from anything."

Like my dream. Stay planted and don't escape when afraid.

Alexis stands and shakes the dirt off her skirt. "I'll check on you later. Maybe a door will open by then."

"Maybe."

She turns to leave, then swivels again toward me. "And for what it's worth, Sam likes you, too."

A hundred butterflies must've found their way into my stomach. He likes me. He likes me? His letters gave hints of affection toward me, but Alexis' words reassure. He likes me.

Picking up a nearby daisy, I pluck each petal. It appears childish, but what better option do I have while waiting for an open door? When the last petal ends at "he likes me not," I toss it aside. "Silly game." I fold my arms and close my eyes, drifting to sleep against the tree trunk. When I wake, it is dark outside and bright stars are winking. Someone placed a blanket over me, and a bowl of bean soup that's cold to the touch rests nearby.

When my stomach growls, I scarf all the bowl's contents. Still no open door. What now? I was sure Elohim wanted this. Maybe I'll find one when Dad is better and the Lesaries start moving again. A bigger tree has to be somewhere up ahead.

I should sleep in my tent for the night. Already, my back is in protest from the hard bark. Instead, I lay on the ground and wrap myself in the blanket. The air feels refreshing and cool. Comfort swaddles me as I rest and marvel at the vast display of stars. Years ago, as Sam and I watched the sky while in the woods near Moon City, he said, "As Elohim's children, we are like stars. So many, yet each just as spectacular in all its brightness."

I see myself shining like a star, brilliant yet with reservation. What if I fail? If I fall, will Sam be there to catch me? My chance might vanish before an opportunity arises.

Surely Elohim won't let me fail when I'm unsure how to reach Sam. He must have a way.

During the night, I dream I am a star. I am content in the sky, living my purpose to be light. But when I slip, I feel as if gravity no longer wants to hold me. I fall fast toward the earth, then crash and dissolve into a thousand pieces. I am dark matter. I am dust.

A silhouette of a man draws near. He digs into the dirt around me and lifts my form into his hands. Exhales. A gentle breeze touches my face, leaving a trace of mint and iris in the air.

"Live," he says.

Like dust forming a whirlwind's core, the pieces of me form, becoming whole.

You were never broken, Elohim says.

Then the voice of Dr. Carper: "A fall doesn't last forever."

Light pours out from me, and I stretch into the shape of a door.

"Take my hand." Cathena is next to me, whispering in my ear.

I reach out, then wake up with a gasp as an electric current ripples through my skin. I *am* awake, right?

A tunnel of light surrounds us. My hand clings to Cathena's. We bolt through the tunnel, like a jet flying through clouds, then land on grass that smells like Earth.

11

———

KEEP

PERO

A gust of wind pushes me back, and I hold on to Cathena's arm. We lean forward against the wind, ready for battle. I'm fully awake, aware I'm on Earth. Though I can hardly see past a thick haze, I catch glimpses of the grass and feel the mud squish beneath my shoes. The air has a crisp bite to it, and although Origo holds some similarities in texture and smell, the very substance of Earth's surface is soil. We must be in Green Meadow and have entered the storm.

"The weather is worse than I expected." My voice carries with the wind, then a torrent pours from the heavens. I'm soaked within seconds. "Just got worse."

"What?" Cathena shouts near my ear.

I draw closer to Cathena. "Where do we go from here?"

"What?"

I hold up my hands in a questioning gesture and shrug my shoulders.

"Where's Sam?" she asks.

"I thought you knew!"

"What?"

I give up. Cathena will direct me somewhere safe, I'm sure.

"This way!" She tugs at my arm, then suddenly pulls me down to the ground as a small branch flies over my head.

My eyes widen in disbelief. "You saved my life!"

"I'm not sure!"

She can't understand me. Cathena would've said something clever or kind if she had. Who gave *me* such good hearing? Couldn't have been from Carper.

We stagger forward, though it's unclear where. The air is dense, making it difficult to see ahead. I guess Cathena's vision compensates for her poor hearing because she seems certain of exactly where to step. I'm tossed around as she avoids what must be nature-ish things I could stumble over.

Like I just did. *Dumb log.*

"Careful!" Cathena helps me to my feet and tugs me into the storm.

I don't see a barn until I nearly run into it. Is clumsiness a genetic trait? I must've gotten that one from my bio dad. Chuckling, I tell myself to stop this nonsense. Not as fun to tease Carper without him here.

Cathena and I enter the barn and lean our weight against the door to push it closed. The wind flattens my wet clothes against my body and slaps pieces of hair against my face. When we finally seal the door shut, the wind leaves with it, like a cat's been scratching my arm and has suddenly retreated. Relief.

The wind howls, and the rain slams against the barn outside. Yet we are safe. I pull back my hair and collapse to a sitting position on the floor. My pulse is high, breath hitched into short, quick pants. "That was bad."

"You gonna make it?" Cathena's hands rest against her knees, and she looks down to study me. She isn't breathing as hard as I am.

"Yep." I lay on my back and bend my knees, feet planted on the floor. I don't care that my drenched clothes are sticking to dirt and straw. "Any idea where we are?"

"Green Meadow. Sam's land. This is Faith's room."

I glance in her direction. "Our Faith?"

"The very one. She must've flown off because when I returned to check on her, she was gone."

"Is this where you disappeared to?" My posture slumps. My worries about Cathena and Sam were unnecessary if she was just vibing with a very large, feathered companion.

Cathena brings over a bucket of water from the corner of the barn. "No. I stopped by here to say bye to Faith before heading for town." She dips her hands into the water and draws it to her mouth. Then she carries the bucket near me.

"Thanks." I sit up. The water is clear. From the barn roof, a slow, thin stream of water drips near where Cathena found her bucket. I drink a couple of handfuls. The liquid is cold, bringing an icy blast to my body. Cathena didn't tell me where she came from before stopping by the barn to say goodbye to Faith or her reason for heading to town. Should I be concerned that she'd leave out the one detail I'm obviously insecure about? I shake again. "Cool."

"You are not cool about this, Pero."

"Actually, I am more than cool. I'm freezing."

Cathena rolls her eyes, then tosses a nearby blanket to me and takes one for herself.

"You seem familiar with this place."

"Relax. I was around for less than 24 hours."

"In the barn?"

"In Sam's house."

"Cool." My teeth chatter.

Cathena groans. "Pero, you're being weird. Nothing happened for you to be jealous about."

"I believe you, but you can't say it wasn't awkward for you to be alone in a good-looking man's house overnight. Bahar met Salmon the same way. They were married soon after."

"Sam told me the same thing."

I furrow my brow. "Sam asked you to marry him?"

"No!" She lowers her voice. "Look, can we drop this?"

"Sure." A welcomed wave of heat washes over me. I shouldn't be angry. It wasn't like she could control where she was transported next. "I'm sorry, Cathena. I'm not sure why I reacted that way."

"Forgiven, but I think you're aware of what this is all about. It's obvious that you two are in love with each other."

I blush. "So embarrassing."

"Shouldn't be. I called it when you two first met."

"You weren't there when we first met." Or was she? It couldn't have been when I traveled back in time and tried to stop Bahar from taking Ruth—me—when I was a baby. Sam forgot the encounter, which is a relief because the whole thing was quite bizarre. Our first meeting felt more like a collision. Henry introduced me to Sam when they came to help me escape from inside the wall of Moon City, in Bahar's room. We were on the rooftop, surrounded by Carper's *lí* plants. The clear glass walls and ceiling prohibited us from leaving except for a circular tube that the Warriors used to fly in and out of. We had to climb instead of flying out since we weren't Warriors and weren't on the plants. Henry teased me. *Scared your boyfriend will fall?* That was before Henry told me he loved me, before I had a crush on Henry in return, which eventually turned into a first love. Yet while Henry and I had fun and cherished our friendship, our relationship never carried as much chemistry as when Sam and I met. An instant felt like eternity. At one point, we feared our connection meant we were related. I almost lost him then. Thank Elohim that little detail got sorted out. It turned out we had a complicated parental situation. Who doesn't? At least we weren't siblings.

"Yep, I saw everything," she says.

I shake my head to clear my thoughts, then focus on Cathena. "Didn't notice."

Cathena laughs. "You couldn't have seen the guards themselves if they'd arrested you."

"That obvious, huh?" I smile.

"When we ran into each other in the woods, you wondered how I found the necklace you'd buried on the roof."

"Right. I remember you watched us from your rooftop."

"Like I've said before, I notice everything."

"What did you notice about me and Sam when we first met?"

"You couldn't tear your eyes away from each other, and when you managed to, it looked like someone had ripped your hearts out of you. Henry seemed to notice, as well."

I grimace. Cathena and Henry's breakup wasn't too long ago. "He's not jealous anymore."

"No, he's not." Her voice sounds sad, like she's unsure.

"Ready to talk about it?"

Cathena shakes her head. "This isn't about me. Right now, we need to find Faith and Sam."

"Shouldn't he be at his house?"

"I checked there during the storm. They were both gone, and Sam's house was destroyed. It's a big, crumbled mess."

My pulse escalates to near panic. "What if he's in there? He could be hurt."

"I checked the house before its destruction. Empty."

I sigh. "Any leads at all?"

"No, but I have someone in mind who can help us figure it out."

"I thought everyone in Green Meadow evacuated."

"So did I." Cathena nudges her head toward the back of the barn. "Follow me."

We approach a trapdoor, and Cathena pulls on the string to open the solid wood panel. An opening reveals a basement below. Is that a fluorescent light shining from the bottom of the stairs? And furniture? It must be more than a storm shelter.

"A hideout on Jimmy's former property has Carper's name written all over it. Who else buys luxurious white couches?"

"Good guess. I doubt Sam even knows about this place. Someone covered the trap door with hay."

"How'd you find the entrance if it was so well hidden?"

"Wouldn't have if your dad himself hadn't come out of it."

I gasp. "Which one?"

"Not Matthew."

"Oh, you mean the snarky, classy father who, for some reason, I love to pieces even though it doesn't seem like it because I'm snarky too?"

"The very one." She moves her arm out to display the entrance. "Pero, welcome to another hidden lab belonging to the ex-famous scientist of multiple universes, Dr. Calvin Carper."

I start down the ladder. "Let the adventure begin."

12

CRY

PERO

A white table displays perfectly aligned vials, microscopes, and trays. A lamp hanging from the ceiling brightens Carper's steady hand. With acute focus, he uses a pipette to transfer blue liquid from one beaker to the next, then smiles when he spots us.

"*Xīn gān bǎo bèi!*" Carper calls me the term of endearment that Chinese parents say to their children. It literally means *heart and liver*. It also means *my heart and soul*. I prefer the non-literal definition.

Carper stretches his arms wide, encircling me into an embrace.

"*Nǐ hǎo, Bàba.*" Does calling him the Mandarin name for *Dad* make me bi-lingual? "How many hidden labs do you have, anyway?"

Carper pulls back, then cocks his head. "Do you mean in America, China, Nauru, or Origo?"

"How many labs on Origo?"

"Zero." He laughs. "Before the shout destroyed it, Moon City was the only."

"Thank Elohim you've settled for this planet." I cross my arms. "Where on Earth is Nauru?"

"A small island in the South Pacific, the least visited destination on Earth."

"Sounds like one of my other dad's historical facts."

"You lucky girl. Few teens have two sets of parents."

"Okay, Boomer. In the U.S., most teens have more than one set of parents. Also, I'm not exactly a teen anymore."

"Right. What, are you eighteen now?"

I chuckle. "Try twenty-two."

Carper frowns. "Not possible."

"It is when I've been living in another universe."

He shares a warm smile, then turns his attention to Cathena. "Glad to see you made it back. Now, let's find some dry clothes for you both. You're drenched."

A shiver races through me.

Carper exits into a closet, then reappears with sweatpants, t-shirts, and lab coats. "They're not pretty."

Cathena shrugs before taking a bundle from Carper. She holds up the shirt. On the front, blue and green membranes float behind bars while the words above the image say *Cells in Cells.* "Did you make this?"

"Leftover swag from fans." Carper hands me the other stack of clothes.

I hold up the t-shirt. "That is the cheesiest thing I've seen."

Cathena frowns at me.

"Good thing I like cheese." I smile. Once again, Carper finds a way to bring out the twelve-year-old in me.

Cathena enters the closet to change first.

Carper washes his hands, then sits on the white couch.

"Sam told me you left for China to escape the storm," I say.

"I was planning on it, but I couldn't leave him by himself. Not when I figured I might have a solution to stopping the storms. So, I hid in here instead of leaving. Didn't want him to be concerned about my safety."

"Have you found anything useful?"

Cathena returns from inside the closet. "Your turn."

I nod, then address Carper. "We'll talk after I change. I'm getting colder by the minute."

The closet—large enough to function as a bedroom—is immaculate. Shelves hold boxes with labels on the front, each marked with names and alphabetized. I halt when I spot the name *Bahar Moshe*. Carper hasn't experimented on Mom for years. I grimace. Mom must've stayed here with Carper before he started acting like a saint. Then why hasn't he thrown out the boxes?

I dress quickly before taking down a box from the shelf before I can convince myself it's a bad idea. When I pull the lid off, I gasp. Atop a pile of documents lies a photo of Mom, the same age as when I discovered her within the Forbidden City walls, waiting for me to rescue. She might be a little younger in this photo, seventeen perhaps. In the picture, long, black hair splays over a shoulder. She does not smile. Her brown eyes look straight ahead, as if she's getting a mugshot before a life-sentence. She wasn't certain if she'd be rescued, let alone by her future daughter. Twice. When the picture was taken, she was Dr. Carper's slave, and he used her as he pleased. She had powerful blood. Special blood. How I wish she didn't!

I hold the photo close to my chest, using the other hand to open a file. The first paper includes Mom's personal information:

Name: Bahar Abram
Title: Subject 1 (S1)
Date of Birth: August 19, 1983
Gender: Female
Experimental Start Date: April 27, 2001

Notes: Prophesied, chosen. Blood Power (BP) is at 230V & 50 Hz frequency, respectively. Evaluating feather pendant to determine any contributing sources. Therefore, S1 contains fragile and possibly hazardous properties. Power Level (PL) to be examined. Replication of properties will be determined in Section 1 (Sec1). DO NOT UNDER ANY CIRCUMSTANCES TOUCH OR HARM SUBJECT 1 WITHOUT DR. CALVIN CARPER'S VERBAL AND WRITTEN CONSENT. See Bylaw 7 in File A.

Interesting. Dr. Carper protected Mom from harm? She told me he'd used her, had done things to her she didn't want me to hear about. Cathena once mentioned that Carper had taken advantage of her. I assumed she meant he'd sexually abused Mom, but how can I be sure? Nausea forms in my gut, though I forgave Carper long ago. Perhaps it's better not to discover the cold, hard facts.

I place Mom's photo aside and flip through the papers, suddenly desperate to find any evidence that Carper wasn't as bad as I've heard. Stacks of reports show details of Carper's experiments on Mom. After glancing through vitals and health charts, I stop at an entry in Carper's handwriting. The date at the top reads *1/11/2002*.

Defilement of S1 noted on December tenth, two-thousand-and-one, at approximately 11:42pm. S1 was previously unharmed up to this point. The court sentenced the convict to death for trespassing in the lab's domain and harming S1. Re-evaluation of PL necessary. Restart from Sec2.1.

Bile rises in my throat. Carper hadn't yet hurt Mom, but some jerk did. I shouldn't have read it. I pushed those details deep into my mind, hoping they would stay hidden, but here they are resurfacing. So close I can nearly see the agony Mom had to endure. Closing the file, I slam the lid on the box. A single piece of paper drops from the shelf to the floor. I pick it up before unfolding the four creases. It is Carper's writing once again but less formal, like he was in a hurry to write the message down before someone found the evidence. I should toss it, forget that it seemed to beg I read its contents.

Off the record, it says at the top. I must read the truth, even if the pain of knowing twists the knife already lodged in my gut. But can I still love Carper once I do?

I read.

It is in good conscience that I can say I have not hurt Bahar physically, yet my resistance wanes as she has run off. I'll most likely begin again after her discovery. Evidence leads to somewhere in the Pacific Northwestern portion of the U.S. and presently includes the extra baggage of a husband and daughter. I can't guarantee Bahar's safety once I find her and her precious brat. The last two years yielded nothing.

I crumple the letter into a ball, tightening it with my fist. Growling, I stomp to the closet door and force it open. It collides against the wall with a thump.

Carper yelps.

Cathena does not. "What took you so long?"

Carper's face loses color as he notices my own, which I'm sure has moved from shades of pink to purple.

"The files," he says.

I nod, then throw the wadded piece of paper at his face.

He flinches, but his sorrowful eyes remain on me.

"What's this about, Pero?" Cathena asks.

I cross my arms. "Only a note about Carper's precious brat."

Carper reaches for the paper, then unfolds it. After a quick scan, he nods, then tears it into tiny pieces. "We've been through too much together, Pero. You know how I feel about you now."

My voice hitches. "Do I?" The past shrouds my memories, like a storm cloud taking over clear skies. I understand why his daughter Cherry still struggles to forgive him.

"You are not a brat, but you *are* precious." He throws the confetti into a trashcan nearby, then looks at me once more. "*Wǒ ài nǐ.*"

"Say it in English."

He doesn't even blink. "I love you. I refuse to let an ounce of who I was then stand in the way of who I am today. Haven't I proved myself by now?"

My face softens, shoulders drop. "Why do you keep her files?"

"For the formulas."

"Why?" I trust him, but when this kind of thing comes up, I'm uncertain if I should.

"Theoretically, a combination of pure blood and positively charged particles dissipates negative cloud charges and concurrently elevates the dew point." He waits as if I understood any word he said and should be excited about what this means.

"In simple terms?"

"The chosen's blood can stop the storms."

Cathena laughs. "Are you the one who stopped the storm earlier?"

Carper nods. "For a few hours, the power came back on using fermented samples from Bahar."

"You're still using her?" I mean it as a question, but it comes out of my mouth in a sarcastic tone and with a catch. I clear my throat. Why am I so jumpy? I'm sure he has some valid explanation for keeping a part of my mother around.

"It's not like that, Pero. I'm using what I already have stored to save Green Meadow. So you don't have to risk your life to save Sam."

"Then why am I here?"

"Pero, just vibe." Cathena holds her hand out toward me. "Don't you see how this could be a positive thing?"

I take a deep breath. Sam is missing while Carper is taking over my mission. "Not yet."

"Carper pausing the storm, even for a little while, gives us a chance to find Sam without being blown away. Plus, because I didn't stop the storm, the misunderstanding about me answering Sam's prayer was resolved. I couldn't change the weather; I was more of a helper in the middle of chaos."

I shrug. "Makes sense."

"Of course it does!" Cathena's wide smile recharges my sour mood.

"So, are we okay?" Carper points between us, his brows knit close together.

"Yeah." I think I'm telling the truth.

"I expect you to be angry," Carper says. "I would be more concerned if you were never upset about the past. But please understand how much it means to me when you forgive. Makes it easier to forgive myself."

I nod, then give him a hug. He smells like cinnamon and fennel, a foreign yet comforting scent for a dad. "I want that for you."

"Thanks, kid."

Now that I'm older, him calling me *kid* doesn't seem so bad.

Carper rubs his hands together. "Let's get to work then. Chances are, we're not finding a way out of this place until that storm stops."

From the basement, the wind outside is a distant howl.

"How has Sam survived?" I immediately regret asking the question. What if Sam is no longer alive?

"Elohim's protection," Cathena says.

My knotted neck muscles unwind. Sam's alive. Elohim wouldn't stop protecting him the second I arrived.

Cathena and I spend the rest of the afternoon as Carper's assistants. By the end of the day, I learn enough scientific terminology to proudly wear my cells in cells t-shirt.

Every thirty minutes, we check the barn to see if Faith or Sam returned. So far, nothing. The couple of occasions we peeked outside brought such a turbulence of wind and rain that it took all three of us to close the barn doors. Carper's right. We're stuck inside until we figure this out.

After serving dehydrated foods for dinner and dismissing us to be done for the evening, Carper finds a spark.

Then another.

"Yes!" Carper leaps in the air, his arms stretching out to form a "V" in victory.

Cathena and I sit up from the two twin-size air mattresses Carper laid out for us.

"What happened?" Cathena asks.

When he doesn't respond but stays focused on his concoction, I turn to Cathena. "Dr. Frankenstein found a heart for his monster."

Cathena shakes her head.

"Fine." I smirk. "The cells escaped their cells."

Cathena ignores me, a grin on her face. "Pero's on fire, Carper. Please explain what's happening or she'll never stop."

"He's happy because he positively found an electron."

Cathena rolls her eyes at me.

"He told a chemistry joke but got no reaction."

Cathena cackles. "Now that's funny."

"Pull the door open for me." Carper adjusts his goggles, then picks up a hand-sized rocket and rushes to the ladder. Sparks burst and cackle from the rocket.

Cathena's already at the top, pushing the trapdoor open, and moving out of the way.

"Got it?" I follow Carper as he balances the launcher in one hand and holds onto the ladder with the other.

Reaching the barn, he remains quiet until setting down the rocket, then opening the sliding door. "Pero, try to cover the flame without getting burned."

I shuffle back two steps. "Are you really stopping the storm to keep me away from danger? Because that seems pretty...."

"Do it!"

"You bet." I hover my hands over the sparklers as best as I can, though I doubt my thin body can protect a few sparks from the fierce elements.

Cathena runs to Carper's side, pulling along with him. The door slides open, inviting a gust of wind through. I resist moving my hands away from the rocket to cover myself from the cold. Hope this works. Seems kind of ridiculous that such a tiny fire would stop a storm. Maybe Carper's delusional and I'm babysitting a missile for nothing.

Carper rushes over to me, picks up the rocket. "Pero, keep your hands around as I carry it. Steady." He walks backward. "That's it."

When we reach the door, Carper slips through, and the wind flings the tips of his hair up like a spiky porcupine. I withhold a chuckle. Now's not a laughing moment.

As I follow through the door, my hair slaps my face. I close my eyes against the air's sting.

"Pero!" Cathena's voice rings loudly.

Squinting my eyes open, I don't know how I stepped away from my duty. Cathena's taken over my spot to protect the missile. Carper lowers it, the flame somehow staying ignited.

"Forgot the key!" Carper runs into the barn. The controller he returns with holds a flashing red button, the key locked inside. "Ready for ignition! Everyone, back up!"

Carper leads us through the barn, shutting the door behind him.

"Whew!" I'm drenched again, wishing for a new cells-in-cells shirt. "Now what?"

"We wait for lightning." Carper sits on a pile of hay, oblivious that his hair looks like a bolt has already touched it.

"High school labs were never this exciting," I say.

Cathena sits, her wind-tossed tresses looking ready for a photo-shoot. "If Carper taught you, they might've been."

Carper grunts. "Pero, I watched your science teacher. Mr. Howard, right? He couldn't tell you the difference between DNA and RNA."

"When did you watch my high school teacher? You realize how creepy that sounds?"

"How else would I have found you?"

I smack my forehead. "Oh, my gosh! I knew you were at my school. Henry never saw you, but I swear I did."

"That really is creepy," Cathena says.

"What can I say?" He shrugs. "I was a jerk then."

"What are you now?" I ask.

"Still trying to figure that out, Pero."

A flash of lightning brightens the room. With wide eyes, Carper jumps up, then presses the flashing red button on the controller. An exploding sound shakes the walls and blasts the barn door open.

I scream, covering my face with my arms.

Rain splats against us, the wind doesn't let up its screeching, and thunder shakes the ground, but no one is hurt. Lowering my arms, I jolt as another bolt of lightning allows us to see the rocket burned to a crisp. The glass of formula Carper placed inside the missile shattered, a billow of smoke twisting in the wind.

Our hard work is done, yet the storm rages on.

Without a single word, we rush to our hideout under the floorboards, change into warm clothes, and settle on our mattresses for the night.

Defeated.

I sort through several words I could say to awaken the fire in our souls that we thought could make anything possible. But the flame is out, along with my hope.

I dwell in the dark until I'm certain my roommates are asleep. Then, I cry.

13

WAKE

SAM

A wail.

I awaken and jolt to a sitting position on a wet rock. To my right is a cavern wall. To my left, a waterfall mists my face. I rub my head, wiping away the damp. Where was I? I rode Faith in the storm, searching for Cathena. Visibility was poor. I hit my head on a tree, then blacked out. Yet Elohim saved me once more and brought me to a secure rock within the beautiful shelter of a place I call *The Cave*.

I've weathered numerous storms in this hidden haven, yet how I arrive here remains a mystery. Escape is impossible. Unlike Cathena and Henry, I'm not a transporter, but somehow I am transported by Elohim. I have yet to find the cave's entrance and exit. I might be in Origo for all I know. The cave itself is large with rocks that stretch tall and a deep pool of water below. The slab I wake up on lies near the edge of the drop-off. A waterfall sends strong currents plunging into the black abyss. The high ceiling is alive with thousands of clinging glowworms, pulsating in waves of neon blue. The slab is the perfect size for a black bear to hibernate alone. Faith would fit in here without touching the ceiling, but her body would be too large for comfort. I'll find her in the barn when I'm home, without a single scorched feather or bent beak.

Whenever I'm in The Cave, I spend my first day admiring glowworms, followed by contemplating whether I should again try to find a way out. But from my times in The Cave, I've gathered that I am here for a reason. When I wake up the next morning, Elohim has carried me to my house. I see no one physically move me. Somehow, I'm here one morning, then in my bed the next. Even through the fiercest storms, Elohim is faithful to keep me safe. But today is my second morning here, the air thick with an energy that seems to pulsate power like an electric current.

I am doing something new, something unheard of. Even now, it sprouts and grows and matures.

Those are the words Elohim spoke in my dream, the very ones He shared with a Lesarien prophet decades ago. Perhaps the new thing is that Elohim hasn't brought me home.

Pero was at the end of last night's dream, like usual. But this cry expressed pain.

I close my eyes. *Elohim, why am I here?*

Another wail.

Opening my eyes, I jump to my feet and scan the walls of the cave. Pero can't be here, yet the sound continues so close, it's as if she's..... Could she be inside the walls?

I swipe my hands against the wet, hard slab. Nothing gives way or sinks in.

After I pound on the wall, I rest my ear against the surface. The voice isn't in the rock.

Straightening, I turn in a slow circle with my hands out to feel the air. I meet nothing, yet it is something. Her voice is present, riding along on sound waves. Alive. Near.

Why are you crying, Ruth? How do I find you?

Pero

Teardrops are like rain. Relentless. Cold. Pounding, yet refreshing. I'm lying on the cot in a shelter which also holds Carper's lab. I am crying, but am unsure why except that I feel defeated. But it's more than that. Perhaps the ground hopes for a season of rain before it can thrive under the sun's kiss.

Elohim, I don't understand these tears. Am I upset about Sam or Dad? Am I tired?

Most likely.

As I wipe another tear from my eye, the storm stops.

Sam

The crying stops.

"*You can trust nature.*" Cathena's words from Elohim repeat in my thoughts. I still don't understand the meaning, but when a wind nearly knocks me off my feet and a crumbling noise roars in my ears, I get it. The Cave is moving, yet I will be safe.

A crash echoes across the cavern's walls. I tuck my head in for cover as debris washes over me. My cheek stings in the very place I once had a scar. When the rockfall subsides, I see a light at the bottom of a pool. A small plot of land lies near the cavern's mouth. On the land's edge, a tree sparkles, as if wearing a skirt of fireflies. An open door shape, brighter inside, is visible on the tree trunk.

I howl in victory. Elohim made a way out!

Below the waterfall, the water appears deep. I could jump. As I prepare to leap, the wind speeds up, pushing me down.

Is that a sign, Elohim?

I pick myself up and walk toward the edge. Again, the wind knocks me over. My tailbone can't handle much more of this.

I can trust nature. Got it.

So, I stay put.

Pero

"How'd it stop?" Carper turns on the light.

"What's happening?" Cathena blinks her eyes open and sits up. "Pero, are you crying?"

"I was." I wipe away more tears.

"Looks like you still are. What's wrong?"

"The storm stopped." Carper stands, then puts on his house slippers.

"Is that why you're crying?" Cathena keeps her focus on me.

"I'm going to check it out." Carper starts for the ladder.

"Carper!" Cathena's hands go to her hips. "Pero's crying."

He turns around, then stiffly pats me on the shoulder, as if he learned how to bring comfort from an AI search. "Why are you crying, Pero?"

"No idea." I dab at my eyes. OMG, will I ever stop?

"Is it...you know, girl stuff?"

I roll my eyes. "No, it's not girl stuff."

"Is it because of the letter I wrote years ago that I tore up to pieces because I really don't like remembering I was such a horrible person?"

I shrug. These are good tears, I think, but maybe I should cry about my dad, too.

Cathena glares. "She has no clue why she's crying, Carper."

He sighs heavily, as if he's never been patient with the female species, then walks over to sit next to me. "How can I help?"

"I'm fine." I look up to the ceiling to blink away any more unnecessary water fountains from my eyes. "See?"

The sound of rain and wind reaches our ears.

Carper swears under his breath.

"Why'd it start again?" I ask.

"The better question is, why'd it stop?"

Cathena gasps.

We look at her, waiting.

"You can trust nature."

Maybe if I don't respond, she'll explain more.

"It was a word that Elohim told me to share with Sam, but I didn't understand it. When Pero cried, the storm stopped. Elohim hears your cries, Pero. He knows what they mean."

"What *do* they mean?"

"That Elohim hears you. He knows some groanings are too deep for words, so He intercedes for you. Cries for you. To trust in nature means you can trust in His Spirit."

"I don't get it."

"You will." In a flash, Cathena disappears.

Carper rushes over to where Cathena stood seconds ago. "Where'd she go?"

I laugh. "No logical explanation. She's done with her mission and is more likely in Origo."

"Weird." When he can't find a trace of Cathena around the room, he looks over at me. "Will you try crying again to see if the storm stops?"

"I can't cry on command."

"Sure you can. Open my archived charts from the closet, and you'll be in tears within five minutes."

"I'd rather live with the rain than open those files again."

"Understandable."

"But I don't think your experiments are the answer, either. Seems to me like..." A gentle breeze floats through the room. I quiver in submission. Tears fill my eyes. I can't help but sink to my knees. "Elohim's here," I whisper.

Carper glances around nervously, as if he's searching for a ghost. "You sure?"

The storm outside quiets down.

Silence.

I close my eyes, focusing on the awesome presence of a Holy God. He is close, like a breath. A whisper. An invitation to experience, know, believe.

Even with my eyes closed, I see a light in a vision. It brightens, consuming all darkness. I am living in light, with light. He is light.

"Pero, look!"

My eyes flutter open and follow where Carper's pointing.

A door is lit before us. It didn't come from a song or guitar, but our tears—mine and Elohim's.

Elohim is for me.

Elohim prays on my behalf.

He hears me cry.

"It's for me." A smile tugs at the corners of my mouth as I step forward into the light.

14

RISE

PERO

Grass *is* greener on the other side. I step through the door and find myself twenty feet from a house. Based on the one remaining wall and a mound of rubble, I guess it's Sam's place. The air feels different on the other side of the storm. The grass is damp, the dirt springing with tiny green buds. Butterflies search for nectar, as if sensing it's near. Life is returning.

I hear a call, like a distant mirage for my ears. Or is that my imagination, beckoning his voice?

"Sam?" I rush to the demolished building and lift a board with two hands. Underneath, drywall coats the concrete floor. How do I get through this mess?

Dropping the board, I wipe chalky hands on my shirt, then evaluate my next step. He may be among larger boards in the center.

When I step forward, my foot hooks on a wooden beam at the edge of the foundation. I stumble, catching myself before landing on the ground. I'm about to take another step when I feel an invisible force pushing me.

"I'm taking a step." A careful look around me shows no one

near. "I'm about to place my foot on the ground." When no one answers and my balancing leg wobbles, I set my foot down.

Nothing.

As I lift my other foot, the wind knocks me off my feet. Is this what Cathena referred to when she said you could trust in nature? It seems the wind has its own personality, or perhaps Elohim is speaking. Regardless, something or someone prevents me from going through the rubble. Which means either Sam's not in this mess, or...something else.

Releasing a small puff of air, I stand and turn to leave. A tingle trails down my spine. The air thickens with an invisible presence. A breeze picks up, causing fallen branches and leaves to shuffle along the ground. I tuck flying strands of hair behind my ears.

"Carper, are you here?" Of course he can't hear me, but since we're both on Sam's property, does Carper also feel the change in the weather?

Where do I go from here? No one calls for me; no one listens. Hot tears trail down my face. *Elohim, why bring me here only for me to be alone?*

The wind pushes me toward a plot of land behind the house. Rows of bare and torn-up soil tell me it was once a garden. Above me, no rain clouds threaten to darken the skies. This isn't another storm. It's not an ordinary spring day either. When I'm near the center of the garden, the wind stops.

I pause. The sun emerges from behind a cloud and spreads warmth over me. I close my eyes, letting the heat fill me. Perhaps I'm taking root, like a watered seed.

I open my eyes. Panic rises in my chest. From the distance, a figure walks toward me. The curved shape informs me its a woman. Her gait is calm and somehow familiar. I gasp when a recent memory flashes across my mind. She's the shadow in my dreams! Should I flee? A tugging within and the measured gentleness of her stride, tells me to stay. This person, whoever she may be, is for me. Besides, when I try to take a step back, I'm incapable. Surely, I'm supposed to meet her.

A moment later, the uncertainty of if I belong here, the terror of wondering what lied beyond that open door from Carper's lab...those are replaced with an assurance that this is my moment. A day to be daring and look myself in the eye.

Because the woman before me, is me.

She's beautiful.

My body trembles, aching to understand why I thought those words, curious if the image of myself before me wonders the same. I reach out a shaky hand, and she mirrors me. I pull back, suddenly afraid. What is it like to meet myself? Will I like her? Will I find myself lacking, wishing to live within the skin of another?

I lift my hand again—hers echoing the same—until our fingers collide. She is like a lost shadow, joints merging until we are one.

"Why are you here?" I whisper.

She doesn't copy my words, her lips not in sync with my own. Instead she listens, a smile crinkling her face. "To show who you are."

I clench my eyes shut, then open them again. She's still present.

"And who am I?" I ask.

Her smile spreads, and I wonder if my grin always displays such a lovely glimpse of joy.

"You know who you are."

I do?

Yes, I do. "I am beautiful. I am loved. I am...."

"His," she finishes. "You are Elohim's daughter, His bride, His chosen."

A lifetime spent searching for my mom, birth parents, Sam are all wiped away in one transformational moment.

I find her. She's beautiful.

"Sing," she says. "Worship opens doors." Then she's gone.

I reach out for the empty space where she stood, as if I can snatch whispers of this version of myself from the breeze, let her be the new me. But I *am* her. I am everything I reminded myself that I am. Or was this Elohim reminding me?

Years ago, when Sam and I searched for a door to open in Origo, Elohim asked Sam to plant his guitar. It was a small sacrifice, yet it symbolized what Elohim requested. A song. Our worship was an offering. From the sacrifice we had buried, Elohim grew a tree with an open door. I didn't step through because I was afraid.

Now, I trust.

Now, I sing.

"You called me. You chose me. I am yours."

In front of my eyes, something beautiful grows from the soil. A single blue iris sparkles in the sunlight. I crouch for a closer look. The blue petals shimmer like fairy dust.

"Is this the sacrifice, Elohim?" Like the guitar was for Sam. I touch the green stem, then pull my hand back when it turns black. "I killed it."

A shovel lies next to the dying flower. Why else would it be here for but to dig? Careful not to further destroy the iris, I push the shovel into the dirt and lift the mound. It takes two more scoops for the flower to be dug up. The iris lies on the shovel, roots exposed and equally as black. Blue petals slowly darken to match the stem.

Surely Elohim won't grow a door from something so tarnished. When a door opened before, Sam had made the guitar with his own hands. The wood was beautiful and without a single blemish. A dying flower can't be what Elohim uses, yet there's fertile soil and a shovel nearby. "What should I plant that you would use to direct me, Elohim? What do I give to you?"

Give me yourself.

I plop down to sit. "You don't mean to bury myself, do you?"

No answer. Yet it was an answer. My thoughts turn to Alexis' words. *I don't see you rushing into or away from anything.* I am to be planted, to be immovable so that He can grow me.

If I believed in Elohim and He knew what He was doing, I must bring my faith to action. Even if it cost me my life. After all, Elohim had enough power to raise me from the dead.

Would He let it get that far?

I swallow hard, a knot in my stomach tightening. I picture the American dollar bill with one sentence written on the back. Very few remember the words and maybe even less believe them, yet they remain: *In Elohim, we trust.*

Easy to say; harder to do.

I carefully move the flower, then dig with the shovel. With every plunge into the dirt, I'm more convinced I'm the sacrifice. Instinct, or knowing, or the pounding of my heart, perhaps, urges me forward. A small voice deep inside me whispers, *A living sacrifice is true worship.* Why? I'm no different from the dying iris. Beautiful yet imperfect, quick to weaken from adversity's touch.

While sores form on my hands, resolve gives me strength. As sweat pools on my back, peace roots itself in my heart. "In Elohim, I trust. In Elohim, I trust."

An hour later, I peer into a small hole. My next action is foolish. Really, no one should try this at home. I take a deep breath, then step in. The surface of the earth lands mid-calf. *Is this enough, Elohim?* At this rate, I'll be finished at my own funeral. *If* I don't die today. A chill travels down my spine.

The earth beneath my feet shifts like quicksand. A roar trembles the ground, making me stumble, but I'm stuck. My body sinks as if someone below is tugging me with a lasso. Dirt spurts outward like a sprinkler. I scream. Holding onto the ground, I use all my upper body strength to pull myself up. I drop lower, the soil swallowing my knees, thighs, then torso.

"Help!" I yell out. Panic sets in. What if I was wrong? Maybe I walked into a death trap and some creep nearby laughs that I fell for their evil scheme.

"Somebody, help me!" I burst into tears. I don't want to—

The ground dissipates. I plummet, shrieking till I collapse with a thud below. A perfectly round hole surrounds me, as if sculpted by hand with my size in mind. I cough, then slowly stand. A bruise throbs on my leg, but otherwise I don't feel any injuries. No way am I escaping on my own.

"I'm here, Elohim!" I shout to the clear sky above. "Do as you wish." Whether He rescues or buries me, so be it. He can make me grow. He can make me into someone more beautiful than I am on my own.

I hug myself, waiting for dirt to rain from heaven and over my head. When nothing happens, I doubt my conviction that this was a good idea. Now what?

"Pero!"

I jolt, then see Carper.

"Is this where the door took you?" He crosses his arms. "You're going to get yourself killed."

"I don't want to die, but I think you're supposed to bury me."

"Ridiculous." Carper gets on his knees and lends me a hand. "You're not a kid at the beach."

I hold on to his hand, but resist the urge to let him lift me up. "I'm serious, *Bàba*. Elohim intends for me to be buried. He said so Himself."

He raises his brows. "Elohim doesn't want to kill you."

"He won't, which is why He'll provide a way out before that happens."

"I am the answer to you getting out, silly girl." Carper lies on his stomach, reaching further down. "Please, grab my hand before I... I threaten you with something terrible."

"You're too nice to be mean now."

"Enough of the games, Pero." His voice strains.

I shake my head. "Remember when Sam, you, and I were trying to find a way out of Origo? Mr. Rose waited for us to open a door."

Carper groans. "I remember. We buried a guitar, and it grew into a tree with a door you refused to go through."

"Yes." I squirm, feeling more claustrophobic by the second. "Well, this is one of those moments."

His eyes widen. "Are you saying you should bury yourself for a door to open?"

"You got it." I push confidence with my voice. "This time, I'm going through it."

"You already went through a door from my lab."

"And it led me to believe for another one."

"You're crazy, *Bǎo bèi*."

"I know."

Carper rubs his face. "Fine."

"Thank you."

"But it'll take hours, perhaps days, for me to cover you." He sighs. "As soon as you're all the way buried, I'm pulling you out."

"Thank you, again."

"I can't believe I'm doing this." Carper leaves for a moment, then returns with a full shovel, face grim. "Hold your breath."

He waits for me to close my eyes, then throws the dirt over me. I cough, covering my face.

"Are you okay?" His pitch is higher.

I spit out bland, dusty soil. Smells like rain but feels gritty against my tongue. "A little dirt won't hurt me." I smile. Inside, my gut is twisting into knots at the thought of what is coming. A lot will hurt me.

Carper starts up the song we sang together while Rose kept us hostage in the Forbidden City. We were, in a way, also buried underground then. Carper's singing waivers, as if he's hiding a river of tears.

While Carper fills his shovel with another mound, I join him singing.

"I surrender all to You. Whatever You want me to do, I will do."

A song provided escape in the past. Elohim rescued us from Moon City and the Forbidden City, and He could do it again.

Carper throws in another shovelful, wiping tears from his eyes. He won't hurt me, which brings no doubt in my mind that his love for me is genuine. All I can do is accept him for the father he strives to be. Imperfectly caring.

Before his sixth attempt to pour dirt over my head, a voice rings out.

Calvin!

Carper moves the shovel aside, then sinks to his knees. He's trembling, head tilted down. "Yes, Elohim?"

Don't hurt your daughter! Get her out of the pit. I see your faith.

Carper bows his head, then sobs.

I look up at the sky, my body about to collapse in relief. "*Bàba*, can you help me out of here?"

Carper dries the remaining tears with his sleeve, then lays down on the ground, his arms extended out to me.

Using the hole's edge, I pull myself up. Slipping, I land right where I started. "I can't reach you."

"I realized that as I was baptizing you with dirt." Carper scoots forward until he closes the distance between us.

"Don't hurt yourself."

Carper scoots backward while lifting me up. Holding onto his arms, I sink my feet into the packed dirt with every pause. Finally, I arrive at the edge of the hole.

"You're as light as a feather," he says.

I finish climbing, then rest, breathing deeply. "I've heard that before." I shake dirt from my hair.

Carper's next to me, massaging his neck.

"You've hurt yourself."

"Nah." His brows furrow. "For a second, I believed He might let you die, then I remembered Elohim's unlike Moon City's god. He doesn't take life; He brings it."

A smile spreads wide. I carry breath in my lungs because of Elohim. Even if He never opened a door for me to find Sam, I'm confident in His faithfulness.

"Look." Carper's quiet voice fills with wonder.

I follow where he's pointing, then laugh. "He provided a sacrifice."

We watch as the stem of the little flower changes from black to green. The tangled roots morph to a healthy brown. The petals close together but stay a vibrant blue. "Let's plant it." I hesitate to touch the iris, but when I do, the color doesn't fade.

I make all things new.

Yes, He did.

Bringing the iris over to Carper, we fill up the large hole.

"The Lesaries told me a story at sanctuary when I was a boy. I forgot about it until now."

I stretch. I'd also have an injured neck by the end of this day. "What's the story?"

"It's about a Lesarien man named Abe who lived many generations ago. One of Sam's relatives, if I'm not mistaken."

I perk up at the mention of Sam's name. If Carper notices, he doesn't let on.

"Well, the story goes Abe was a good friend of Elohim's, and one day Elohim tested Abe's faith. Elohim asked Abe to sacrifice his son."

"So, what happened?"

"Elohim stopped Abe right before he was about to plunge a knife into his son's chest."

I grimace. "Makes being buried sound less painful."

"If a father receives an order to kill or even hurt his child, any method is terrible."

A shiver passes through me. I could've died if Elohim hadn't pulled through. But I didn't. Surely, He was looking out for me.

After we fill the hole and plant the iris, we anticipate something to happen. The iris seems to shimmer more, as if it too expects a wonder.

Carper folds his arms. "In Chinese culture, a blue iris symbolizes faith and hope."

I glance his way, then to the flower. "Seriously?"

"Irises also are symbolic of spring and change."

"Dang, that's cool." I fold my arms, suppressing a yawn. "Do you think we'll see the flower change soon?"

"Likely."

Five minutes later, the petals grow. The blue, tear-dropped pieces—so delicate and soft—unfold to reveal tiny stems, like little antennas announcing the birth of something new. In the center of the pistil is a window, and from that window pours bright light, inviting me forward.

It's not a door, but it *is* an entrance. I don't hesitate to enter.

15

HOLD

SAM

The singing stopped roughly thirty minutes ago, but there was no mistaking Pero's voice: strong, pure, with hints of a bluesy rasp.

Lyrics still echo in my head. *"Whatever you want me to do, I will do."* Something special is happening, even if I can't see it.

I try to stand, but Elohim, or whatever unseen servant He's sent, pushes against me so hard that it's impossible to move. I don't feel pain; more an invisible force blocking my way. The tingle trailing down my spine and the goosebumps on my flesh tell me to believe. Elohim must want me to rest and watch as He prepares a way. I wait in expectation.

How should I respond when I find Pero? A kiss seems too eager; a hug too informal. Unless it's a full hug, not one of those side-hugs that friends give when they don't like an invasion into their personal space or avoid giving the wrong impression. Forget the hug thing. More than likely, she'll feel as awkward as I will. Knowing the prophecy involving me and Pero feels like entering an arranged marriage. The prophecy said Elohim would fulfill His promise to bring a Messiah by joining chosen people together in marriage.

When I first met Pero, she had traveled back in time to rescue the Lesaries. It was right before Henry and I left for Moon City to rescue Bahar and where I'd meet her once again. Pero said I wouldn't remember our second encounter in Moon City's walls because we were living in the past, but I recall every little detail of that moment and the next. How could I not? The chemistry between us made every interaction strained. Do engaged couples from family arrangements dream about their betrothed? Do they have a say in the arrangement? Pero could easily dismiss the prophecy and our attraction and peace out.

Butterflies in my stomach rush me back to when I was sixteen and couldn't form a logical sentence in the presence of a cute girl.

Sam, stop taking yourself so seriously. Laugh a little.

I force a chuckle and rub my face. A grown man can approach a woman with respect and dignity. A kiss on the hand? Too medieval. A handshake? Pero offered one once, but I turned it into a hand hold instead. Her trembling in my grip must've been a good thing, because she wasn't the first to let go.

A hand hold it is.

At the sound of tumbling rocks below, I stand. *Am I able to move?* I shuffle my feet, then step forward. I *can* move! When the shuffling noise continues, I peer over the waterfall. I catch movement near the open door of light. In front of the tree, rising from where water meets land, I find her.

My stomach knots. I recognize the slim waist and coffee-brown hair landing right above her delicate shoulders. Pero steps away from the water, squeezing out the remains from the bottom of her pants. I can't peal my eyes away from her. Cathena was attractive with her looks and kind personality, but when I see Pero.... She is radiant.

The light from the tree seems to follow her every move, as if it too notices she is one of the chosen. Pero lays a petite hand against the bark. Hours in the Origo sun has darkened her otherwise porcelain skin into a light beige. She laughs boldly, head bent back. I could dive into that laugh, let all the joy stirring inside fuel me into a blessed man.

"Where have you brought me now?" Her voice carries across the distance.

Pero has yet to look my way. It seems she's asking Elohim based on the sense of awe in her tone. A smile stays on her lips as she scans the cave's perimeters. When she spots me, the expression dissipates.

"Who's there?" Her shaky voice echoes against the cave walls.

Blinking rapidly, I shake off my stupor. I should've said something right away. Instead, I stood in the shadows, gawking at her. So much for respect. "I...." Where are my words?

"Sam?" She shields her eyes.

"Yes." I squeak out the word, then swallow hard. I feel sixteen again, and I can't blame it on hormones anymore. Or can I? "I'm coming to you."

"Okay." Pero moves to one side of the tiny piece of land. "I'll check for the best way for you to climb down. These rocks seem steady—"

"I can't wait that long." Stepping toward the edge of the waterfall, I remove my shoes, then dive into the pool of water below. Glowworms hug the bottom of the water hole, providing a blue light on my way up. When I break the surface, I swim toward the edge, then stand when my feet land on pebbles.

Still five feet away, Pero moves her hands from her pockets to her hips, then settles on taking a strand of hair and twirling. Her nervous habit appears more obvious with shorter hair. "I wasn't expecting you to jump."

My feet trudge through the shallow waters to draw closer. How bad would it be if I took her into my arms and gave her what I'm certain would be the best kiss of our lives? Would she pull away? Because my mind is consumed by the idea of having her near.

Beautiful, precious woman.

I am one foot away from her when I force myself to stop. "Hi."

"Hi," she whispers back.

She's lost her voice, too. Her eyes seem unsure where to land as she searches my face, until she finally matches my stare. She is confident, showing a mature side of her, both new and intriguing.

"I'm Sam." I use the same greeting I've used previously, followed by a wink, in case she doesn't recall the inside joke between us.

Pero extends her hand and releases that infectious laugh. "I'm Ruth."

"Ruth." Taking her hand, I hold on like before.

Again, the tremble beneath her skin, but now accompanied with a hitch in her breath.

"You don't prefer I call you *Pero*?"

Still holding on. The warmth in my chest travels through my whole body and to my fingertips.

"You say my birth name as if it's the key to something wonderful."

"It is." I whisper her name, then move closer. Reaching a hand toward her hair, I pause and watch her expression, waiting for permission. When she doesn't hesitate, I let my fingers gently touch a strand as smooth as silk. A jolt of energy passes through me, and I shudder. "Do you feel this?"

She nods her head. Her gaze flickers to my lips, sparks pooling in her eyes like embers. "I wasn't sure if it was me at seventeen, but today I'm positive it's always been real."

I dare to draw even closer, my face merely inches from hers. The air between our lips pulsates like a magnetic charge.

"Sam?" Her voice is thick and sultry.

"Yeah?" One inch more.

She steps back.

I snap to attention. Did I dream that we'd almost kissed? Was I imagining that she desired to as much as I?

She shakes her head, retreating until her back rests against the tree. She glances at the open door as if contemplating whether she should run through it.

Why am I rushing? "I'm sorry, Ruth. I shouldn't have assumed anything."

"Please, don't apologize." She averts her attention, the look more familiar from when she was a teen. "I didn't plan for things to progress so quickly. I'd like to get to know you without going straight into what comes naturally to us."

I raise a brow. "Naturally?"

"We're attracted to each other, obviously."

Her bluntness brings a grin to my face.

"I was hoping to spend more time kissing and less time talking." Her face turns a shade of pink, but she doesn't stop. "The other way around. Not that I don't want, you know, but that's not what I meant. Let's talk more. I mean, like, check in, if that makes sense."

"It does." *Not at all.* I prefer other ways to learn about her, but I suppose conversation is the respectful and right way to start a relationship. A lifelong commitment requires more than romance. Pero is right about her convictions, which makes me desire her more. Her intention was to suggest *less* time kissing and not none at all.

For the moment, my impulse tells me to get out of here. How many hours will I last in an intimate cave, alone with the woman of my dreams?

16

REVEAL

PERO

The near-kiss has my head spinning. Did that really happen? I resist dipping a hand into the water to cool my flushed face. Over-talking earlier was embarrassing enough. *I want to spend more time kissing.* My face grows hotter at the thought of it. Why do I say such stupid things?

"Ready?" He stands by the open door, hand extended.

The light reveals a fresh, deep cut on his cheek, shaped identically to the scar he once had. How did I not notice it before? "You're bleeding."

Sam touches the surface of his face, then examines the tinge of red on his fingertips. "Only a little."

"Seems like a whole lot more than a little." He's still drenched from diving into the pool of water, illuminating the wound. "I don't have anything to help." I'd happily give him my *Cells in Cells* shirt if I could.

Turning around, Sam removes his shirt, as if that will make me less distracted by his bare back, toned and swarthy. With no shirt, no shoes, and brown cargo pants, he resembles a good ole boy from an American country music song. A wave of heat rushes through me. Can I look at this man without feeling touched by an angel? I avert my gaze as he turns again and presses the shirt against his face.

"Is that better?"

After a quick glance at the cloth on his cheek, I nod, then step away. "Ready to leave this place?"

Out of the corner of my eye, I see him grin. Why do I get so embarrassed about this kind of stuff?

"Ready." Sam joins my side and touches my hand. When I don't pull away, he interlaces his fingers with mine. I give him a smile, then remember why I wasn't going to look at him. Too late. The muscles along his chest and ribcage are well-defined. *Shoot.* Why couldn't he have some excess weight or a distasteful tattoo to make it easy for my eyes to look away? I force myself to focus ahead. "By the way, when we get out of here, Carper will be on your property."

"Great! It'll be nice to see him again."

How will Carper react when Sam appears like this?

When I don't respond, Sam pulls his shirt on.

"Oh, no. Don't do that." *Wow, I sounded way too eager.*

"Wouldn't want to distract you too much." Sam winks. "I'm sure we'll find something for the injury when we reach Carper."

We step into the exit. When we land, we're not in the field, and Carper's not leaning against a shovel with brows raised at my flushed cheeks. Rather, we're standing on the slab above the waterfall, back in the cave. We are also wearing different outfits, as if we emerged from REI's closet. Jogger pants, long-sleeve shirts, and fleece jackets. Waterproof hiking boots cover our feet, and a sling bag drapes around one shoulder.

What the heck?

As real as the thousands of blue glowing things above my head, we are stuck at the top of a waterfall and appear like we're ready to go touch grass.

"What are those?" I crane my neck for a better view of the ceiling.

When Sam doesn't answer, I watch him search along the cave's walls. He places a hand into a nook and tugs. I wonder if it hurts his mind to be that focused without verbally processing. My brain would definitely explode with all that silence. Yet he is talking inside. I can sense it in his furrowed brow and gentle "hmm" sound he mustn't realize he's making. Oh, well. I'll let him think his way through the situation while I settle in. I'm okay with staying in a cave for a little while.

Sitting on a nearby rock, I peer over the edge. "The drop's a lot longer from this angle. I would've been scared to death jumping off this thing."

Sam remains focused on the task.

"What are you thinking?"

"I'm wondering why we can't leave through this open door."

"What I want to figure out is how an open door gave me a whole new style." I zip open the sling bag and find lip gloss, mints, and a hairbrush. I chuckle. Maybe it's a sign I should get over myself and kiss the guy. Not that I follow advice from trees.

Sam looks behind the nook in the wall, then straightens. "There must be another way out."

"What's the hurry? A magical cave is the perfect place to chat."

"After you've been here a couple of days, you'll feel claustrophobic."

The ceiling can't be over more than fifteen feet tall, and the area above the waterfall matches the size of my old house in Green Meadow. "It's cozy." I stand on the rock for a closer look at the ceiling. "Plus, we can watch the glowing blue stuff." When Sam and I stargazed, their beauty was enhanced as I cherished the thrill of lying next to Sam. Lying under a blanket of whatever covers the ceiling above me sounds even more exhilarating.

"They're glowworms."

"Really?" Up close, they look like a string of beads. "Will they drop on us?"

"Not likely." Sam crosses his arms.

From the shadows, I can't see the cut on his face anymore. I take a step toward him, then stop when he puts his arms out as if warning me to stay away.

"Are you mad at me?" I ask.

"Why would I be?"

"I don't know. You're acting weird."

"I'm not acting weird."

"Are we arguing?" I'd hate for our first argument to be over glowworms.

"No." He sighs. "This isn't the way I'd imagined us meeting. I thought having both of us here would stop the storm, but we're trapped. Nothing is working."

"The storm stopped."

"Briefly, yes, but then it started again, so you can't be the one to stop all this." He rubs his temple. "Maybe the prophecy was wrong."

"Are you saying you don't think I'm part of the chosen?" I ask.

"I'm not sure what to think."

"Sam, the storm stopped."

He perks up. "For longer than a few hours?"

I nod. "I made it stop."

"Really?" Sam's posture stills. For one marvelous moment, his eyes stay locked on mine. Then he draws closer.

He hovers over me, his hand placed against the rock where I sit. The cut on his cheek is definitely gone, but I can't seem to form the words to tell him. His face pauses inches from mine. How did he get this near? One second he's leaning against the wall, while the next has him a breath away from my lips.

I swallow the lump in my throat.

In that fragile pause, I anticipate the right moment to break our defenses. To embrace love and seal it with a vow. Sam has always been the one. He's like a lighthouse, drawing me in, saving me from any other choice. "I've searched for you. Even when I didn't realize."

Sam smiles, then sits next to me on the rock.

I exhale and let the tension between us do the talking.

Sam rubs his jaw, then looks at his hand. "I don't see any blood. Is the wound still there?" He turns to show the side of his face.

"It's gone." I brush my fingertips against his cheek where the blood and cut have completely vanished. A shiver passes through me as I graze against the rugged stubble. When his breath hitches, I drop my hand quickly.

Sam nods toward the tree below that still holds an open arch with light pouring through. "Elohim has used something planted to heal me before. The tree didn't take us somewhere else, but it seems like it caused healing."

"Where do you think the cut came from? Looks like the same place you had a scar once."

"Probably from the branch I hit before blacking out and waking up here." His brows furrow in concentration. "Come to think of it, the cut *was* in the same place. I wonder why that is."

I shrug. "Could be coincidence."

Sam's eyes brighten. "I have an idea before we try getting out of here again."

"You always were the man with a plan." Part of the reason Sam and I are a great pair is, while I have the drive to take action, Sam thinks things through.

"We have the supplies to stay here. I'd say let's catch up, get some sleep, then check out the door after resting."

"Yas! Let's do it."

"Wait." Sam holds his hand up as if to stop me from getting too excited. "There are two rules."

"Are they easy enough to follow?"

"I'll let you be the judge. I sleep near the tree, and you sleep here."

I give him a playful smile. "What if *I* want to sleep near the tree?"

"Fine with me."

"I was teasing you, Sam. I don't mind sleeping up here."

"Right. I'm happy to change spots if you'd like."

"Really, I'll be fine." He's nice, but is he almost too nice? I guess there are worse qualities. "What's the other rule?"

"In a moment, I'll sit over there." Sam points to another rock five feet away. "While you stay."

"That's your rule?"

"If we're going to be together for a while, I can't be near you."

"Why's that?"

"Because all I want to do is kiss you."

Holding my breath, I wish he'd act on his blunt statement. Afraid that he will. "Then why haven't you moved away from me yet?"

"I will in three seconds."

I retrain the desire that rushes through my blood. "One."

He positions himself in front of me. "I have two seconds."

"Two." My voice turns quiet and serious. I tell myself to move, but I'm grounded to my spot. "Three."

For a brief moment, he leans in. This is the moment. A shiver trails down my spine and makes it to my toes. Then—he stands.

I blink rapidly and clear my throat. Rejection feels like a quick jab to the heart.

Sam moves over to the other rock and sits. He looks off into the distance. "It's nothing against you."

"What is it then?" I think Sam doesn't want our relationship to move too quickly, but how can I be certain?

After a moment, when I begin to think he won't utter another word, he speaks. "I'd like to let Elohim write our love story, and part of that involves following His guidance. I think it would be best for us to respect boundaries before marriage."

I nod. Since following Lesarien practice, I've learned that Elohim's best intentions for romantic relationships involve waiting for sex before marriage. From what I've been taught, waiting to have sex teaches patience, commitment, and respect. In high school, many classmates boasted about who and how often they did "it" with, yet they never seemed fulfilled. I've compared their casual and fleeting relationships against the Lesaries' committed ones. The difference is staggering. The majority of Lesaries who follow Elohim's guidance in abstinence are stronger for their endurance.

"I think setting boundaries will help make this happen," he says.

I nod again, thrilled the reason he hadn't kissed me wasn't because he didn't desire me. "How?"

"We can create rules and determine to stick with them, but it will be nearly impossible using our own strength. Let's allow Elohim's Spirit to empower us to live out our convictions."

How often had I tried to do things on my own, but saw breakthroughs when I quit trying to gain control?

Sam leads us into a prayer so personal and beautiful that my eyes water. I crave this man's leadership. His wisdom promises far and wonderful things that I refuse to miss out on.

"How are you feeling?" he asks.

Rarely have I had so few words, and not in a bad way. Sam offers direction and encouragement, then waits to hear my thoughts, hopes, and fears. Can a man get any better than this?

"I'll be transparent," I say. "I'm working on my anxiety."

"You've had plenty of reason to fear in the past."

He's right. Between a mom-swap, a recovered abusive birth father, a dad who watched me like a hawk growing up, and enough near-death experiences to put me in a therapist's office, it's logical for me to be anxious. "It wasn't reasonable for me to fear coming here."

"Sure it was. I asked you to give up everything based on Elohim telling me you could stop a storm. That takes a lot of faith, Ruth. I'm grateful you stepped out like that. Is that all you're worried about?"

"At this moment, it feels right to be with you, but based on past experiences, I can't always trust my feelings."

"Have you asked what Elohim thinks?"

"Yes. I also talked with Shea and Bahar. That's why I'm nervous. Everything lines up to me being here with you, yet I worry about what's next. Am I ready for a committed relationship? Can I make you happy? Will you make me happy?"

"Which is why we're talking, to figure all this out. The truth is, we'll never be completely ready for big decisions. There are moments to step out and believe Elohim will give us strength and endurance along the way."

Another nugget of truth to tuck into my heart. "What are your fears? Or is Sam Nesim ever afraid?"

"I'm not perfect." Sam clears his throat as if he's uncomfortable about opening up but will do it, anyway. "When my dad died, I wondered why Elohim would allow my mom to be alone. Their marriage was like no other I've ever seen. They loved each other deeply."

Sam's mom, Bahar, ended up raising me when she disappeared from Sam's life. While Bahar and my dad, Matthew, have a great marriage, I never saw a connection as strong as the one Sam described between Bahar and her first husband.

"I sense a similar bond between us as there was between my parents," Sam says. "But I've already lost you far too often."

Three occasions pop into my head: when I was young and taken with Mom, as Henry's girlfriend, and when Sam left to claim Jimmy's property and I took off to find Mom in China.

"In the middle of all three separations," Sam continues, "I believe Elohim challenged me to let go of you and hold on to Him. You are His first. Since He's led me to you, I'm honestly nervous to jump forward. What if I put everything on the line, only to lose you again?"

I shake my head, conviction stirring through my thoughts and rising with my voice. "I'm not *Pero*, the girl you lost. I'm *Ruth*, the one Elohim is returning."

"You believe the prophecy is true, then?"

"Yes." Never have I been so certain. I ache to embrace this calling Elohim Himself brought before me. To serve another human being with love, compassion, friendship, and trust. "I'm in."

"Very good." Sam chuckles. "Me too."

Minutes freeze when you don't have a clock. We talk for what could be hours, exposing our worries, hopes, and dreams and discussing our favorite flavors, music, and sports. I'm completely content with learning everything I can about him.

Finally, when I think it's impossible for us to ever stop talking, Sam's eyelids start to draw shut while he lists his preference for resolving conflicts. Then, he completely nods off.

Either he can fall asleep easily or I'm boring. I doubt that since he fell asleep to his own voice. I cross over to him and nudge him so he can lie down. He jerks awake.

"I need sleep." His voice is groggy.

"Don't move. I promise to stay away from you."

He nods and lays down on the hard floor. The poor man has been sleeping on a rock for a few days, but he falls asleep without any complaints.

I'd sell my social security number to sleep that easily. I shift behind the rock, giving Sam space, yet remaining close enough to feel safe. Finding the coziest spot possible—which is really the flattest looking slab—I lie down. My fleece jacket is warm enough to ward off the damp air. Watching from my back, I see the glowworms above. Their string-like forms are mysterious. It's incredible how something so thin and radiant could be full of life.

I reflect on my first date with Sam. We don't banter, and he doesn't always catch onto my sarcasm. He's warm, caring, insightful, honest. Maybe that's exactly what I long for. Someone to balance my passion and spontaneity, to calm my anxieties. They say opposites attract, but I also could see opposites being like a finished puzzle. Pieces united to make a whole.

I can't sleep.

Sitting up, I open the mysterious bag beside me. While looking for the lip gloss, my hand finds a thin piece of material. I grip the object, then pull it out. A letter! My heartbeat races as I open the folded paper. In the center is my feather pendant, attached to a new chain. Such a familiar object brings comfort, and I can wear it again thanks to whoever fixed it. After putting on the necklace, I read the signatures on two pieces of paper. One from Shea and one from Mom. Is Dad okay? Did Cathena make it back safely?

I read Shea's first.

Pero, remember to inhale.

Shea

Short but impactful. Taking his advice, I take a deep breath before plunging into Mom's note.

Hi Pero,

I couldn't go with you to find Sam because I sensed this was your journey. Your dad is feeling better, and we're finally on the move again.

As I was praying for you, I had the sense that when you

do find Sam—which I believe you will—you should follow the age-old Lesarien custom. You probably haven't heard this one before, and I'm sorry that I can't tell you what it means. I will someday, I promise. When Sam is sleeping, remove the blanket from over his feet and lie next to him. Once he wakes up and finds you there, ask him to spread the corner of his blanket over you and tell him that he's your guardian. He'll explain more. This will sound bizarre, but I seldom ask anything of you. Trust Elohim in this.

I'm including your feather pendant, which your dad fixed. You must've dropped it on your way out, and I thought you might wear it to remind you of your koach in Elohim.

Love you,
Mom

I inhale once more and feel confusion settle into my lungs. Lay at his feet? That would break our boundary rule. He doesn't even have a blanket. What am I supposed to do, remove his shoes and place my face next to stinky socks? Weird.

With a groan, I stand to my feet. Dad might be feeling better, but what happened to my mother?

17

———————

REST

PERO

Sam breathes softly, sound asleep. This is crazy. Massively cringe worthy. After taking a few steps toward Sam, I rush for my bag, remembering it prepared me for such a time as this. I coat my lips with gloss, run the brush through my hair, and drop a mint into my mouth. No dragon breath allowed in this cave.

Wait—should I bring a mint for Sam? *Too far, Pero.*

When I reach Sam, the first thing I notice is a blanket over him. Where did that come from? I guess I shouldn't question anything at this point. Maybe a dragon *is* in this cave.

With a quick breath, I kneel near his feet. Lying on his back, face relaxed, Sam smiles in his sleep. I don't wish to cause a stir. What if he woke up while I'm staring at him? Talk about creepy.

I slowly remove the blanket from his feet and decide to leave his shoes on for multiple reasons. Using subtle movements, I lower myself until I'm on my side and curled up in a ball near him. I can't believe I'm doing this. What if he kicks in his sleep? Mom better know what she's talking about.

A draft makes me shiver, yet peace follows and settles over me. I'm at rest near Sam, like I could finally fall asleep.

Roughly twenty-two years ago, I somehow appeared at the base of a tree. Alexis says I slept soundly during my nap after having cried for hours. But a heartbeat later, I was no longer safe. It was Mom—Bahar—who picked me up from under the tree. Alexis screamed out to stop and Sam ran toward the two of us, desperate to reach us. Mom saved the past to prepare me for my future with Sam.

A sense of déjà vu washes over me. I'm near an open tree. Not quite asleep, but calmer. Before finding this cave, I cried for hours. Now, I wait—before the supernatural, before the miracle —for Sam to answer my cry. I crave his vow to have me and hold me without ever letting go.

I crave completion.

It's clear now. Lying at Sam's feet means restoration. Not because I'm returning after leaving him behind, but because I am deeply and whole-heartedly his.

18

———————

ENDURE

SAM

Something's wrong. I wake up with a start, sensing someone near. Very near. I can't see clearly, but whoever it is, has curled up at my feet, asleep. Sitting up, I'm covered in a blanket except for my feet. How did this blanket get here, anyway?

"Pero, is that you?" I ask.

The form stirs. "Sorry to startle you." Her voice is raspy, a little shaky. "Uh, as you're my guardian, would you spread the corner of your blanket over me?"

My heart swells with joy. Am I imagining her request? I wasn't aware she knew this Lesarien custom. "Shhh, it's alright."

I rub her arm, feeling the cold skin beneath her jacket. Her small form shivers.

Lifting from the corner, I drape the blanket over her. "Stay here for the night. I'll make the proper arrangements in the morning. You're a kind woman, Ruth."

"I'm also a confused woman, but we'll talk after we get more sleep."

She closes her eyes, and I lay down, scooting to be more

aligned with her. Wouldn't want to accidentally kick her face while she sleeps. What does she mean by confused? Is she aware of what her actions mean?

It takes a while for my racing heart to settle down with her so close to me. I'll make sure to get up quickly when awake, but until then, I welcome the warmth. Best Lesarien tradition ever!

IT MUST BE morning because I feel refreshed and not like I slept on a slab or that my sleep was interrupted by a woman lying next to me. Speaking of said woman, where is Pero? I remove the blanket and stand. Did I dream she laid next to me? After stretching out the kinks in my neck, I walk to the other side of the rock. Pero's not there. Finally, I spot her on the small island next to the tree. From this distance, I can't tell if she sees me or not.

"Good morning," I call.

"Good morning." Her voice is more cheerful than expected, considering Pero is not a morning person. "Are you planning on going for a dive again or should I tell you how easy it is to climb down from the side?"

My pulse spikes thinking about being near her last night. I'm stunned by her actions. Perhaps I could use another plunge to yank me to my senses.

Without a word, I remove my shoes and jump into the water. It's colder today, yet I welcome the sting as I work my way up and out. I approach her, each step closer an agonizing reminder of the rules I set, one of which was broken when we slept next to each other. But does following tradition count as a broken rule?

Elohim, help me.

She grins and shakes her head. "You're fascinating."

Her hair hangs in waves above her shoulders and a glossy sheen covers her lips. "And you're breathtaking."

She tilts her head. *Adorable.*

"Let's make another rule," she says. "No flattery. I really can't stand it."

I wink. "I'll remember that."

She's the first to avert her eyes. "About last night…"

"Right. I recall you saying you're a confused woman. Mind explaining?"

"I don't know what I did."

"You uncovered my feet and laid next to me."

"I remember that, but I don't have any idea what it means."

Disappointment thuds against my chest. Then why did she do it?

"I got a letter from my mom last night." She pulls a piece of paper from out of the bag attached to her, then holds it out toward me. "Please, read."

I accept the letter from her outstretched hand. She bites her lip as if she's nervous. What happened? Is her dad okay? An object against Pero's chest catches my attention. My eyes widen as the feather pendant turns from a dull brown to a bright blue. *No! It can't be.*

Pero must follow my gaze because she yelps, then removes the necklace as if it's a hot coal. She drops it to the ground, then studies it from a distance. "Why's my necklace blue?"

"Did you have it on yesterday?" I would've noticed if she had.

"No. My mom gave it to me with her note."

Right. Maybe what Bahar wrote will connect the pieces between Pero asking me to be her guardian and the blue pendant. I hope not. With trembling fingers, I scan through the letter. It's just as I feared. When I'm done, I hand it back to her. "I see."

Why would Bahar ask her to do this? Pero has no idea what

it means. Bahar mentioned she felt Elohim prompted her to. It was the right moment; I am the right person.

But now I'm not.

My heart beats wildly in my chest. I have to tell her the truth.

"Well?" Pero's face scrunches as if concerned.

"You proposed to me."

Her mouth drops. "That's a proposal? I've got to say, the Lesarien culture is very unromantic."

I chuckle, then sigh. How can I explain this without it coming across as hurtful for both of us? I didn't expect the pendant to turn blue. I assumed we'd be married as soon as possible, but Bahar's letter has me at the edge of my fears, nearly falling into complete panic. Pero needs someone to restore her loss. When a piece of the heart is lost, following Lesarien customs is the way. But does it have to be?

I plunge into the truth. "Long ago, Elohim spoke to the great prophet Ezekiel through a metaphor for the Lesaries. The story was about a girl hurt and unclothed. Elohim told her, 'Live!' and made her grow like a plant in a field. Then He took a corner of His cloak and covered her. He made an oath and sealed a covenant with her, and she became His. But then she deserted Him. Elohim didn't literally marry her; He doesn't desire with the flesh like we do, but in a holy and jealous way.

"The metaphor illustrated the Lesaries' unfaithfulness to Elohim, reminding them of His covenant to restore us on the Day of Atonement. He loves, protects, and longs for His people, like a good husband. Spreading the corner of a garment over someone represents being under His wings. To protect, love, and long for. When you unfolded the blanket from over my feet, you asked for me to be your guardian. Your husband. When I covered you with the corner of the blanket, it symbolized acceptance and a promise to marry you."

Pero smiles. "I changed my mind. That's the best proposal

custom I've ever heard. It also strangely matches what Elohim told me to do before coming here. I planted myself in the field on your property at His command, and He saved me."

My senses become alert. It *was* Elohim's plan for her to approach me, which makes it difficult to tell her the truth. "I'm glad you listened to Elohim, Pero."

"You called me 'Pero.'" Her face scrunches. "You seem to do that when distancing yourself."

"Do I?" I rub my forehead. "This custom's hard to explain, Ruth."

The squeeze of her hand on mine brings warmth. "I'll be okay."

"You're sweet." I take her hand. "It's true that I am a redeemer of our family, fulfilling the prophecy for the chosen three. However, the feather turning blue means someone is preventing you from choosing who to love."

"Like a curse?"

"More like a stronghold. The person preventing you more than likely has no idea that it's caused the feather symbol to change."

Pero lets go of my hand. "I don't understand."

"Someone who fell in love with you in the past holds a piece of your heart. In order to break the stronghold, he has to give you permission to marry me by returning the part of your heart. If he agrees, then we can be engaged to be married. If he doesn't, then only one cure can fix it."

Color drains from Pero's face.

"The Messiah's arrival will fulfill the law," I say.

"I have to sit." Pero plops down on the ground.

I crouch next to her. "Talk to me. What are you thinking?"

"I'm doomed."

"We'll make a way. Once Henry knows we're together, he'll break the stronghold."

She shakes her head. "You don't understand."

"What?"

"The coming Messiah came to me when I was seventeen."

My heart skips a beat. "Are you sure?"

"Cathena saw Him too. He said He'll return one day and would be born through my future descendants. His name was Yeshua."

My shoulders drop in relief. "That's good news. The Messiah will come through the chosen, which means Elohim will make a way for us to be together."

"But, Sam." Tears surface in her eyes. "Cathena and Henry broke up, and Cathena never shared why. I'm afraid. What if Henry isn't willing to return the piece of my heart?"

A chill passes through me. I bring my arms around Pero and hold her. Henry *can't* still want her. Ruth's mine, and I love her.

19

LEAVE

PERO

My palms sweat. This can't be happening. What kind of crazy curse makes you ask for a piece of your heart back from your first love? "Can't we pray for Elohim to break the stronghold? He has all the power."

Sam withdraws from his embrace. "Yes, He does, but He might be allowing this to happen. The Lesaries have a law they've carried back for generations. A couple not destined to be a priest, prophet, or chosen one can marry. However, it's a little trickier for those chosen, or, as in your case, those called to carry the chosen one. Yes, you could choose to marry whomever without breaking any laws, but being married to another chosen means you're compatible. Similar to transporters like Henry and Cathena. Their marriage would dynamically unite them, making them perfect vessels for Elohim's use. For whatever reason, Elohim has allowed Henry to keep your heart. He might still have feelings for you. Could be he hasn't completely let you go."

"What's stopping us from being together, though? Couldn't we marry regardless if he still has a piece of my heart?"

"Wouldn't you rather us enter a relationship without anyone pulling you back?"

"Yes, but can't we get past my previous relationship together?"

"We could." He hesitates. "We would have to live with a blue feather reminding us of what happened. In marriage, I'd be giving you my whole heart, but unless it's restored, yours will never be mine."

I feel a blush trail up my neck. Why did I give another my heart? Now I'm stuck with a dumb curse! Do I regret having loved Henry? In some ways, no. He was fun and a good friend, but did I grow personally through our relationship? Not until our breakup.

"Henry told me he was a transporter *after* we started dating. He never said giving him a part of me created a stronghold over the chosen." Tears stream down my face. "I feel deceived."

When Sam brings his arms around me, a warmth settles in my stomach and my muscles relax. I lay my head against his shoulder. Sheltered. Loved. Whether or not intentional, how dare Henry threaten to take this away!

"You did nothing wrong. It was my responsibility to tell you, too."

"Would I have listened?"

His kiss on the top of my head has me melting.

"Let's not blame anyone. There was nothing wrong with you dating Henry. He's a good guy, even if he's over the top with charming women. Still, I'm confident he'll make everything right." He clears his throat. "Since this has come up, I guess I should ask if you're still holding onto a piece of his heart."

I pull back, observing his expression. I moved on from Henry already. "Do you think I'd be here with you if I did?"

"I thought not. You *did* propose to me."

"I'll do it again." I flash him a smile. "But on purpose."

"Isn't it the man's job to propose in American culture?"

"True. Maybe I'll let you ask the question."

Sam tilts his head and laughs. "I already did!"

I smile. It was the right call to turn him down then. I was young and afraid, but it pains me to remember the rejection I made him go through. He's committed his passion and attention to me for so long.

With a smirk on my lips, I pat the top of his head. "Tag. You're it." My hand sinks down into a pile of thick, black hair. I could let it stay, explore the course texture with my fingertips, but I refrain and lower my hand to my side.

He winks, then lifts my blue feather necklace and puts it around his neck. I stifle tears when I recognize his mercy. By wearing the stronghold, he's carrying my burden. He's owning my pain.

"I'll ask you again," he says. "Mark my words, I'll win trophies for the greatest proposal in history."

"I don't need the greatest proposal," I say. "I just need you."

His eyes brighten before turning dark, his face drawn. "We'll overcome this, Ruth. I believe we will."

I nod. "Elohim's never let us down." Standing, I lift him to his feet. "What do you say we give this magic door another chance?"

"I say 'yes'." He holds my hand, about to step forward through the doorway, then pauses. He scans the cave. "Something changed in the air."

The walls stay put, nothing moves. No danger in sight, but I sense the shift. A pebble near me jumps.

"Did you see that?"

A few more pebbles bounce.

"Yeah." With wide eyes shifting, Sam studies the floor.

A rumble starts from the ground, causing my body to tremble. The shaking increases, the cave seeming to spin me like a tilt-a-whirl ride.

I stumble to clutch on to a nearby boulder. "Is this an earthquake?"

Rocks tumble down the sides of the cave. Dirt rains on our heads. Glowworms from the ceiling drop like a meteor shower. I scream as one of the larvae lands on my cheek.

Sam covers his head with his arm, then shelters me with the other. "We have to get out of here."

"What if the door doesn't work?" I raise my voice above the deafening sound of the cave closing in. My heartbeat races. We'll be swallowed alive if we don't move, but if the door leads to the slab above the waterfall like last time, we'll be crushed.

"Can't stick around to find out!" Sam pulls me forward.

Hand in hand, we step into the tree and land in Green Meadow's field.

"Whew!" I wipe sweat from my brow.

"Are you hurt?" Sam asks.

I shake my head, pulling away the sticky glowworm from my face. After throwing it on the ground, I shiver. "Only mildly disturbed by that slimy thing."

"Thank Elohim we didn't land above the waterfall." Sam wipes the dirt from his hair and clothes.

The storm has cleared. Sunshine blinds my eyes, as warm and comforting as softened cream, its radiance easing over the dripping fringes of my damp shirt. The town I grew up in is free of rain and lightning, the past storm of this field buried under rich soil and rows of flowers. The grass has transformed from charred strands to vibrant greens. In the middle of the garden's soil—an abundance of plants and produce surrounding—the iris I replanted still sparkles. Unlike the cursed feather, the blue petals remind me that a new beginning is ready for harvest.

"We did it," I say.

"Elohim made a way." Sam wraps an arm around me. "He brought you."

20

GATHER

PERO

My favorite man walks beside me, our arms looped together. I place a hand against his solid biceps, relishing strength, treasuring gentleness. Today is blessed.

A thought intrudes my mind, like a cloud covering Green Meadow's sunny skies. We're not here to think about ourselves, settle down, and live happily ever after. We're here to find my ex-boyfriend, as awkward and terrifying as that sounds. Will Henry refuse to grant us peace for our marriage? Will I break his heart all over again by asking him to return mine?

I swallow, noticing a lump in my throat. "How do we find him?"

Sam pats my hand. "Honestly, I expected Henry to have been transported here since Elohim knows we're looking for him. Maybe we should wait in case that happens."

"Much better plan than getting on a fourteen-hour flight to China. As much as I love the country, I'd rather not relive traveling around the Forbidden City with the person who stole my heart." I loosen my grip on Sam's arm.

"It's okay that you dated him, Ruth. I'm not feeling hurt about the past."

I let go of Sam. "Yet you won't accept me without this taken care of."

"I'd feel better if we could resolve this first. Having blessings for our marriage is important to me. I'd like to make sure we've let go of all ties."

"I *have* let go."

"But obviously Henry hasn't."

Goodbye isn't forever for us. Henry's words spoken to me on more than one occasion echo through my mind. Sam's right. It would be better to address this now. Henry should hear about mine and Sam's engagement—if we really are engaged.

Marriage. Such a permanent word, yet being near Sam makes me itch to explore and cherish every part of him for the rest of my life. I never expected such longing for someone. My breakup with Henry had me determined to remain single, at least until I figured out life as an adult on my own. But now, Sam's love will carry my past until it's healed.

"I have an idea," I say.

Sam glances my way. "What's that?"

"Let's head to my old house in Green Meadow and look for a hidden door in the closet. It's the same place my mom traveled. I bet we can find Henry through the opening."

He pauses, brows furrowed. "I'm not sure how I feel about that."

"Why not? There's no door around here, and I'm almost positive no solution in Carper's lab. I wouldn't want him to use his experiments on us, anyway. Half of them don't work."

"True." Sam chuckles, then rubs his neck. "I guess we can try. I haven't been there since the storms, so I can't guarantee it's intact."

It's been years since I've seen the house Dad and I lived in. If the storm hasn't hit it, I wonder if I'll still find my bedroom the way I left it at seventeen-years-old: purple pillows scattered along the bed, cushions to sit on in the closet, with strings of lights hanging from above, my guitar on a stand in the corner. Why is Sam reluctant to go?

With no sign of Faith and a broken-down truck sunk into a mud hole, our best option is to walk. An hour later, my house stands directly in front of us without a blemish in sight. It's smaller than I remember but still as charming. I recall our last goodbye here, uncertain then if it would be our last. I tilt my head back, looking toward the heavens. Grateful.

I skip over the squeaky step leading to the porch and go straight for the entrance. Pausing, a flash of memories flood my mind. Here, starting at this very door, Dad raised me, Mom disappeared, and Henry and I went for a daily run. I used to tune Henry out with music, but he was my loyal bodyguard, a friend at school, a young man willing to lay down his life for me. A transporter who is suppressing me from my future with Sam. I flex my fingers. Should've never removed the earbuds.

Sam steps behind me, so close I could lean back a fraction to lie against him. He places a hand on my arm. I'm happy for it, having no strength of my own to rest.

It dawns on me then. Sam hesitated about me coming here, unsure I was ready for the memories.

"We don't have to go in," he says softly against my ear.

I swallow. As my back grazes his chest, I sense the energy between us, a pulsation holding me from falling backward into fear. I could live in his protection, let his secure arms shelter me from the painful memories beyond this door, but I'll only go one way.

"Onwerto." Turning the handle, I push until the door creaks open to a short hall. The rack to the right holds Dad's trench coat, the same one whose pocket I'd snuck a hand into. I'd retrieved the feather necklace when planning to find Mom on my own. The coat taunts, a reminder of my first reckless gamble with fate. I'd let fear live in this home, then carried it with me.

In my mind's eye, I see myself as a little girl, secure in her daddy's love but wondering what is beyond and why it's too dangerous to find out. Yes, I had a life beyond these walls. I went to school, stores, track meets, choir practice, but always with hawk-like eyes, searching for the one who'd steal me away.

The same night I took the necklace out of Dad's coat, Henry tricked me into coming outside. In Henry's defense, Carper had held a gun to his face. Or at least, that's what he said happened. What if Henry tricked me into being kidnapped? Maybe he's not the guy I thought I knew.

On that same night, Carper stole me from my home, from Dad. Carper and I have come a long way, yet forgiving is not a once-and-done. Right now, with reminders of all the wrongs and difficulties I've endured, it's hard.

"Say the word, and we'll leave." The hush of the empty room must've triggered Sam's whisper.

My instinct returns to a word I repeated in my mind for many years.

Run.

Fear chokes out reasoning until all that's left in my chest is a tight, cold feeling. But I can't open my mouth to say I'm scared or get my feet to flee. I'd rather confront anxiety directly, tell it to go, that it has no right in my presence. I am a child of Elohim, and His power stirs in me. With fists ready to take on my past, I stand strong. *Bring it on.*

Sam leans in from behind me. "This doesn't have to be your battle."

I pause. My defenses loosen their hold, my body relaxing. Why would I reawaken fear?

Hello, anxiety. You can stay here, but you no longer own me. I belong to Elohim now.

I take a shaky breath, then turn to Sam. "This isn't my home anymore."

"I know." His voice dips into a lower tone. "Love has no fear."

My pulse picks up speed. "What are you trying to say?"

"I love you." His gaze is steady, his jaw set.

My knees weaken. A warm shiver travels down my spine. Sam's actions have communicated those three words, but to hear them—oh, to realize they ring true is to experience life!

When I feel as if my feet have finally touched the ground, I grasp Sam's hand. "I—"

"Hello?" A man's voice speaks from the living room.

I jump, and Sam's brows furrow. We're about to peek around the corner of the hall when the person appears, nearly colliding.

Suddenly, I wish I could rewind the last few seconds and quickly tell Sam I love him before it's too late. The first person I loved stands before me. The young hottie has grown into a fully grown man dressed in expensive jeans and t-shirt. Henry's pile of blonde curls and piercing blue eyes are far too gorgeous without considering whether I was in my right mind when I left him.

But you can't judge a man by his cover.

21

SING

SAM

"Pero!" Henry gives her a full-body squeeze as she lunges for a stiff side hug.

"Henry!" I'm unsure of Pero's tone. Is she happy? Shocked? Withholding a punch? Because I am. After he releases Pero—which wasn't soon enough, in my opinion—Henry holds out his hand toward me.

Shaking hands? I don't think so. I grip it before pulling him in for a hug. "We're friends, Henry." At least, we will be again once all this is sorted out.

"Right. It's been a while, so I wasn't sure about your comfort level."

I cross my arms, clenching my teeth. "You seemed sure about Pero's level of comfort."

Henry sizes me up, more than likely evaluating whether I'm a threat. I will myself to calm down.

"What brings you here?" Pero smiles.

We already have the answer, but I'm glad she thought of something to diffuse my sudden fireball.

Why am I so easily jealous? Hadn't I told Pero I was confident Henry would make things right? Besides, they only dated for a few months before breaking up. I understand how Henry could get in and steal her heart that quickly. He's better looking than I am, flamboyant, and far too flirtatious.

"I thought *you'd* be able to tell me why I'm here." Henry keeps his eyes on Pero. "I was transported to you with no obvious message and right when I got off of work. Doesn't look like you're in danger."

Pero grins. "Are you enjoying the medical field, Dr. Beggs?"

The way Pero said *doctor* makes me cringe.

"Lov'n it." Henry leans closer to Pero, still avoiding eye contact with me. "Remember when I helped you with your sprained ankle?"

"How could I forget that dumb hole I fell into?"

If I recall correctly, *Dr. Beggs* wasn't strong enough to carry Pero. But *I* was.

"Anyway, as a doctor, I get paid to fix sprained ankles. It's fire."

Good for him.

Pero offers another smile. "I'm so happy for you, Henry."

"Thanks. But enough about me. How's life, Ro girl? By the way, you look fantastic."

Yeah, he really called Pero by the old nickname he'd given her and complimented her looks while giving *the* body scan. The signal all guys use that means, *Hey, I'm into you.*

Pero's eyelashes flutter. "That's sweet of you to say."

Oh, no you don't. I told the woman of my dreams that I love her, and she's responding to another guy's flattery.

"Things have been good. I'm enjoying—"

Moving close to her side, I place my hand on Pero's back and gaze directly into her eyes. Yes, I'm showing possession. No, I don't care what Henry thinks about it. "Would you be alright with saving this conversation for later? We should talk with Henry."

Her eyes widen for a moment. "Sure." Her voice is shaking.

"Talk about what?" Henry's nervous tone resembles a dad who's questioning his daughter's date.

I answer Pero first. "Are you alright?"

She nods, a blush trailing up her face.

Henry clears his throat. "I'll chill in the living room." He turns and leaves.

Pero quiets her voice. "I don't feel comfortable talking to Henry about returning my heart."

I stroke her arm. "How come?"

"I'm nervous around him." Her face turns a deeper red. "It stirs up too many memories."

"Of your past relationship?"

"Yeah."

I search her eyes. "You don't have feelings for him, right?"

She shakes her head. "Not at all. It's just awkward."

"Should I start the conversation without you?"

She bites her lower lip. "I'll go with you. How bad can it be?"

I guide her into the living room, my hand resting on her back.

Henry stands up from Matthew's glider, fidgeting with his hands. "What's happening?"

Pero and I sit on the couch.

She leans forward, clearing her throat. "I'd like my heart back, please." Her voice is firm, yet carries a subtle tremble.

Henry sits. "I wondered if that was the case."

"Why do you have it?" Her voice hitches.

I rub small circles along her neck, feeling her muscles loosen their hold.

Henry sighs. "Because I might have feelings for you."

"You can't." Tears gather in her eyes. I wish I could punch Henry's stupidly perfect nose and hold her close, but it's important for Pero to sort through this on her own. Offering her comfort can come later. Henry's nose bleed can, too.

He looks between the two of us, then hangs his head. "Because you like Sam?"

"No."

I pause the neck rub, trying to gauge the storm of feelings written on her face. Is she angry, sad, changing her mind about us?

A teardrop falls down her face. I imagine it would feel like warm sea water against my lips.

"I *love* Sam," she says.

My body freezes, a wildly beating heart the only part of me still moving. She loves me. I can't peal my eyes off of her, and I can sense her refraining from doing the same. Finally, she turns her head toward me. Once our gazes lock, we're stuck to this spot, hopefully for eternity.

She loves me.

"Should I leave you two alone...again?" Henry's voice breaks our trance.

I rub my jaw. "So, will you return it?"

"How are you sure she and I aren't supposed to be together?" he asks.

"That's not how it works."

"Why not, Sam? Because of Elohim's *suggestion* that transporters marry each other?"

I stall, waiting for my breathing to regulate before I say something I'll later regret. "What's really going on here, Henry?"

Placing fingers against his temple, he shakes his head. "I've been thinking a lot."

"About what?" I ask.

He mumbles.

"I couldn't hear you."

I glance at Pero, who's turned a shade paler.

"I said my happiness!" Henry's nearly shouting.

The seconds on the grandfather clock echo in the quiet

room. Something is eating at Henry, and it's not only about Pero. Should she be a part of this conversation, or will it hurt her more?

As if reading my thoughts, Pero stands. "Sounds like you two should talk." She leaves.

"I'll be right back," I say to Henry. Jumping to my feet, I follow her to the hall.

She stops mid-step when she senses me but doesn't turn around. "Promise not to beat him up while I'm gone."

I move in front of her. "Depends on what he says."

Worry sets in her eyes, yet I hear a smile in her voice. "I'll be in my room." She walks away.

"Ruth?"

She tilts her head, brown eyes sparkling, hips swiveling as she turns to look at me. "Yeah?"

I'm stuck in my spot, unwilling to move if it means releasing this moment. A perfect picture.

"Did you really mean what you said in there?"

She grins. "That I love you?"

I nod, swallowing the lump forming in my throat.

"With all my heart." She walks backward until reaching the first room on the right.

After she disappears, I let out a lengthy breath. *Have mercy!* A count to five regulates my heart rate enough to find Henry.

He's slouching on the sofa, feet up on the coffee table, head laid back. "You're in love with her."

I sigh, then sit in the glider. "I won't deny it."

Henry lifts his feet from their reclined position and sits up. "You won't give up until she has her heart back, will you?"

"It's not yours to keep."

I study his relaxed posture, but I know better. When Pero's not in the room, it's easier for me to be compassionate toward Henry. I welcome his honesty, even if I don't appreciate hearing it. "Do you care for Pero, or is something else going on?"

"I'm so tired of rules!"

"Henry, I asked if you care for Pero. You were flirting with her earlier. You mentioned you might still have feelings for her."

He places elbows on knees and head against hands. "I've tried to get her out of my mind."

"What about Cathena?"

"I broke up with her."

"Why would you do that?"

"Because she's too perfect."

Couldn't have described her better myself. "In what way?"

"Her body, personality, bravery. Too much confidence is intimidating. Don't tell her I said that."

"Does confidence have to be intimidating?" I ask.

"Yes."

The melodic sound of a guitar floats from Pero's room. The music's tempo is upbeat, the fingerpicking heard from more accomplished musicians. Pero's confidence doesn't intimidate. Rather, it invigorates me to be the best man I can for her and release her for all Elohim has planned.

Now, to win back her heart.

"So, we're repeating history." I curl my hands into fists, then straighten them. "Fighting over the same woman."

"It's no fight," Henry says. "If Pero wants this, then what choice do I have?"

"You'd give her up even though you still have feelings for her?"

Henry twists his hands together. "I'm following your example."

"Explain."

"Years ago," he says, "you let Pero choose between us. You were willing to let her go without any expectations that she'd return. That's sacrifice, man. The real kind of love."

The memory brings an ache in my chest. I felt as if I'd die

when I walked away, but she wasn't mine to hold on to. Now that Elohim returned her to me, I'll fight for her. "Feeling forced to leave isn't the same as forfeiting your rights to her. You're quitting."

"Would you rather me not?" He crosses his arms.

"I'd rather end this conversation with both of us in a good place. Will pretending to return Pero's heart fix whatever is really going on?"

Henry doesn't respond.

"You mentioned you're sick of Elohim's rules. Care to elaborate?"

He stays quiet while the sound of Pero's guitar changes gears to a bluesy tune. "It's really hard not to like you, Sam. She's wise to fall for you."

I clear my throat.

Henry scratches his head. "Yeah, about the rules comment."

From the background, Pero sings about coming home. I've heard this one before. The words ring truer being at her old house. Her home is where Elohim is, not where walls are built or torn down. And in Elohim's house, rules guide and protect.

"We've been friends since we were kids," Henry says.

"Yes, we have."

"You've seen my struggles. I thrive on adventure and don't like settling in one place for very long."

I nod. Henry's ADHD makes him the perfect transporter. Him staying in one place long enough to earn a doctorate's degree and holding a job is impressive. He's matured in many ways.

"When I was dating Pero," he says, "every day was an adventure. At first, she didn't appreciate my spontaneity. Anxiety prevented her from trying a lot of things, but the day she ran past the line that Matthew had told her not to cross because it was too dangerous, she became—I don't know—different. Bold and unstoppable. We had fun together."

I stuff down the jealousy working its way back. This is their story, and while I'll never be a part of it, their relationship served a purpose: to be young and carefree.

"By ignoring the rule about transporters marrying each other," he continues, "I satisfied the longing in me to do something different, experience something new. Being with Cathena was incredible. I couldn't find a better fit for me, yet after a year, I became restless again, feeling like I'd lived a boring life by dating another transporter. I got scared, Sam."

"Of what?"

"Settling for an ordinary life."

"Did your relationship with Cathena feel ordinary?"

Henry chuckles as he looks off into the distance. "Not in the least."

I let him get lost in his thoughts. Now that Pero has stopped playing, I miss her. I'm ready to restore the necklace, grab her hand, and run straight to the nearest officiator. Instead, I wait.

Finally, Henry clears his throat. "I owe you an apology."

I raise a brow.

"I've been holding onto an idea when I should've completely released her. My obsession with Pero was selfish of me and prohibited you from pursuing her fully. I'm sorry."

"Apology accepted." As much as I'd go for pulling Pero's necklace out to get the process over with, I refrain. "I bet someone else would like to hear an apology a lot more."

Henry tilts his head, then his eyes widen in understanding. "How will Cathena ever forgive me?"

"I don't think that'll be a problem. She likes you."

Henry grins like a schoolboy. "Really?"

"She averted the conversation whenever I pried about you two. Isn't that code for a girl liking a guy?"

"How am I supposed to know?"

I shrug. "I thought you understood everything about women."

"Gosh, no. I never had to."

"Right. Because you were a chick magnet."

Henry stands taller. "Precisely."

"That's not exactly the best reputation."

"Hey." He grins widely. "A man's gotta take what he can get."

I nod, a chuckle escaping. "You're not settling, Henry."

"You're right. I'm winning." He stands. "Don't let me interrupt your life with Pero anymore. You have my blessing and my heart."

"I'm grateful." Removing the chain from around my neck, I offer the blue feather pendant, glowing like sapphire.

"Dang. You're sure you wouldn't enjoy that color more?"

"Henry!"

"Joking." He takes the pendant and closes his eyes while giving it a squeeze. "I return Pero's heart, setting her free from all ties of the past. She wholly belongs to whomever she chooses."

I break out into a sweat. She still has to choose. What if after one look at Henry, Pero has changed her mind? Impossible. The way her eyes stayed glued on me as she retreated into her room couldn't convince me otherwise.

The necklace returns to its dull brown, the Lesarien word *koach*, meaning *strength*, etched on the back. After Henry hands it over, I pull the chain over my neck. Bringing my own necklace from out of my pocket, I wear it along with Pero's. Strength pulsates in my veins. We are better together.

"I appreciate it, Henry." I give him a hug, with no animosity.

"Congrats, bro." He releases, then playfully punches my arm.

"You, too." I nod. "I'll get Pero so she can say goodbye before you leave."

"Sounds good."

As soon as I turn around, I hear a whoosh in the air. Behind me, Henry has vanished. I frown. Transporters can't choose when they come and go, but I was hoping for him and Pero to finish sorting things out, too. At least I have good news to bring her.

I do a little dance on my way to Pero's room. Maybe I should've knocked first, but it doesn't make a difference because Pero isn't in there. Is she in the bathroom? Across the hall, the door's open wide, no light on. In her room, I notice the rustled covers on her bed and the window sealed shut, curtains drawn. A couple of steps in, I see it.

A sunken seating cushion lies on the closet floor, with a guitar nearby. Thick light filling an archway against the closet's wall prevents me from seeing what's inside. My heartbeat picks up speed. She's in there somewhere. Lost. Or perhaps a runaway. With the necklaces restored and near my heart, nothing constrains me from pursuing her. Vigor and passion course through my blood, as I run through the open door.

22

FLY

PERO

Inside my bedroom closet, a wave of warmth travels along my spine and light spills around me. I set my guitar down on the floor, then turn to see a doorway forming the closet wall. It's hard to say what's beyond, but the heat feels like comfort wrapping around me.

"Pero." A whisper travels through the empty space.

"Who are you?"

"Who are *you*?" the voice replies, resembling the caterpillar from *Alice in Wonderland*.

My name isn't Alice, and I'd rather not travel into the unknown, yet something pulls me toward the opening, like a magnet attracting metal.

Entranced, I step across the threshold.

Sam moves to the background of my mind as my bedroom fades from view. All around me, light feels similar to water, tastes sweet, smells of blooming flowers. Is this heaven?

From the distance, a figure floats toward me, enlarging with every passing second. I'm not scared, rather I feel nothing at all. Should I?

When it's closer, I notice giant wings flapping. A high-pitched whistle fills the air, sounding like freedom. It's Faith.

Whatever I'm standing on—perhaps nothing—shifts, and I catch myself before tumbling. The atmosphere thins, revealing my feet against a wispy, white cloud, quickly dissipating from under me.

Not risking a chance on a cloud to carry me, I lean forward, arms extended, knees bent. Faith is a heartbeat away when I jump and pull myself up, clinging onto her feathers as she flies forward. Behind me, the cloud disintegrates as Faith flies, the horizon ahead transforming into shades of pink, purple, and blue.

Closing my eyes, I dream of ice cream, kittens, and sailboats. I even think of rainbows and unicorns. Wherever I am, I'd happily settle here forever and never lack anything. Not when make-believe seems tangible, as if I'm actually tasting lollipops from the sky. Sitting up, I stretch my arms wide. The breeze rolls over me like gentle streams of water, filling me, drowning me in bliss. When I sense a cooling and prickly shift in the wind, I open my eyes to see a shining castle made of gold below.

I *must* be in heaven. How had I died? Was it painful? Quick? It feels like I've been here for a while. Years, perhaps.

Faith plunges toward the castle. My hair doesn't fly behind me, nor do my eyes sting. It's as if I'm floating from one part of a white, cloudy paradise to the next.

The eagle lands on a golden path, leading to the castle's entrance. Before me, a gate lies open. Am I an expected guest?

Not a soul in sight. Fear hasn't cautioned me yet, so resembling Alice more with each passing moment, my curiosity pushes me along the path. A marbled staircase stretches wide, giving the castle a modern look. Circular towers reach so high, a mist obscures their tops.

Inside and to my left is a winding staircase. Flowers painted in gold adorn the dome-shaped ceiling. Central to the open foyer, a statue depicts a man in a tailored suit, with hair pulled into a bun. His hands rest on his hips, chin up, chest out. Ahead are three wood doors, each displaying a gold number labeled one through three. Escape room vibes.

Staircase or doors? Which to explore first?

I approach door number one, then knock. When no one replies, I turn the handle and walk inside. A chair sits adjacent to a roaring fire. Victorian lamps make for soft lighting, illuminating tables with stacks of books and loose pieces of sheet music. A small harp stands in the corner of the room. On the opposite side, Carper plays on an upright piano. Yes, the real doc himself is in a room resembling an English professor's office and playing Clare de Lune perfectly. I must be dreaming.

I sneak toward the piano, pinching myself along the way. My bio dad is a brilliant musician?

When I reach the instrument, I use it as a pedestal to rest my elbows on. Carper doesn't acknowledge my presence, fingers flying along the keys. Maintaining a straight posture, his body sways in sync with the tempo. I shake my head in wonder. Just when I thought I knew him.

As the last note fills the air, he pauses as if he too is stunned by whatever magical spell the music had him under.

I clap, and he bows his head.

"You never told me you're such an accomplished pianist."

He blinks and scrunches his face. "You're late for the third week in a row."

"I don't understand."

"Where's your head been, Ruth? Is something going on at home?"

He never calls me by my birth name. "Uh, no. Just the usual walk-like-a-Lesarien jam. Should there be?"

He stands. "Never mind." With a scowl on his face, he inspects around and behind me.

"What?"

"Don't tell me you forgot your guitar."

"My guitar?"

He sighs. "For lessons. Like every other week."

"We're here for lessons." I'm in a stupor, waiting for him to break out in a laugh and tell me he's joking. But clearly, he's not.

"Do you think your mom would be paying one of the top musicians in the world for you to stand here and watch me play piano?"

"Right. My mom paid for you to give me guitar lessons." Something big is up. Like, *dad is an alien and came from a third universe* kind of big. "Can you remind me of my mom's name?"

He places his palm against my forehead. "Temperature's fine. Her name is Alexis. You're her one and only daughter."

At least he's got that partly right, but he didn't mention Bahar, the woman I still call *mom*. "You're still my bio father, right?"

Now he laughs, but it doesn't make me feel any better. "I should've guessed this was about your parents' recent divorce."

When I don't answer, Carper's smile fades. "I don't plan on dating your mom, and if I ever did, I'd make sure to get your permission first."

"Thanks. You're right, I was worried about nothing." Not even close to what I was thinking, but at this point, it seems best to play along. Wherever I am, it's not reality. "Sorry I'm late and forgot my guitar." I nudge my head toward the instrument in the corner. "Can you teach me something new? That harp looks interesting."

"Doesn't work."

"Then why keep it?"

"It was passed down from my family. Some antique from ancient days. It belonged to a famous Lesarien man, or something like that."

I do a double take. "Which man?"

He sighs. "How am I supposed to remember? I never paid attention in sanctuary as a kid. My mother mentioned it could only be played by a future king."

"You?"

He smirks. "Do I look like a king to you?"

Apparently, Carper doesn't remember trying to become king of the Lesaries here on Earth, but what does he mean that it doesn't work? "Can I try playing it?"

"No!"

"Sorry." I raise my hands up in the air. "I'll back away from the harp."

Carper shakes his head while walking over to a rack of guitars. He picks up a 12 string, hands it to me. "I think you're ready." Placing a sheet of music on a stand, he sets it in front of a nearby chair. "Have a seat."

When I sit, he plunges into a monologue about the differences between 12-string and classical acoustics.

Tuning out his monotone voice, I recall the Carper I first knew. The man who spoke with charismatic fervor and let rage and conviction drive him into action. After he became a follower of Elohim, that same passion was used to repair his damaged relationships. *This* life—whether it's an alternate past or redo—seems to have suppressed his very being. Aware of Carper's brilliant mind, it isn't surprising he'd be a skilled musician, yet he's bored, and I can no longer let him be.

"The more strings," he says, "the better harmonics to the guitar's overall sound."

I raise my hand.

He rolls his eyes. "Yes?"

"Have you ever considered becoming a scientist?"

"I beg your pardon." His brows knit.

"I mean, this whole music-professor-with-perfect-piano-fingers looks good on you, but if I'm going to be honest, you seem bored out of your mind."

"What makes you say *scientist*?"

I shrug. "You seem like the inventor type."

"My undergrad was in chemical engineering."

"See? There you go. Finish your doctorate, and quicker than you can say 'I did it' in Chinese, you'll be a doctor of science. You'll be famous for, let's say, extending the human lifespan."

A thought alarms me. Suppose I'm back in time before his career as a scientist? If I'd kept my mouth shut, maybe I could rewrite the past and he wouldn't traffic Mom. But in this scenario, Bahar didn't adopt me, which means Mom is living a normal life with a husband named Salmon and a son named Sam. Which also means to meet Sam, I must persuade Carper to proceed with the experiment. To fulfill the prophecy. Maybe for the second round, he can test the chosen's blood without ruining our lives.

"Just don't torture people while you're experimenting on them," I say. "It's not nice and makes their kids' lives really complicated."

Carper's jaw tightens. "You seem to speak from experience."

"It's quite possible."

After a moment, he stammers on his words. "You won't be learning guitar today, will you?"

Standing up, I place the 12-string in its spot, then return to my seat.

Carper sighs. "Your mom has to start paying me more. I'm not a licensed therapist, you know."

"I didn't say you were." I tilt my head and smile.

"I don't have the hots for your mom, Ruth."

"My weird behavior has nothing to do with your romantic life, but since you mention it, who are you dating at the moment?"

"That's none of your business and not an appropriate

conversation between a music teacher and his fifteen-year-old student."

I choke on saliva. "So young!"

"In fact, why did you close the door?" He swings it wide, revealing a sitting room.

Alexis, *mom*, sits on a couch, absorbed in a book. The peacefulness that softens her face warms my belly. How would have childhood in America been with Alexis as my mom? Apparently, it would've resulted in a divorce between two parents and music lessons with a depressed teacher. I'd say *hi* to Alexis, but she'd be confused as heck, and she's reading *The Hunger Games*. Must I say more?

"I have an open-door policy for a reason," Carper continues. "Can't afford to be sued because a client thinks I'm her shrink."

"You said you're one of the most famous musicians in the world. Wouldn't that make you rich?"

"It was sarcasm." He sits on the piano bench, facing me. "I'm dirt poor."

"You wouldn't be if you were a scientist."

"You're touching a nerve."

"How so?"

"I haven't told my story to many." His voice is quieter.

Here we go.

"I can't believe I'm about to tell you." He spins one of several rings on his fingers.

I zip my lips, then throw away the key. "Your secret's safe with me."

He peers through the door in Alexis's direction, then at me. "I was once on my way toward discovering something huge. It would've changed my life. Really, it would've changed the whole world."

I lean in and whisper. "What happened?"

"Someone found my early studies, claimed them as their own, and had them published."

I gasp, pretending I've never heard. "Terrible!"

"Anyway, they're missing one key ingredient to make the study happen, but I'm not allowed to buy the patent to find out what that ingredient is. I'd face jail for using something no longer mine. Even worse, a man would be after my life."

"Does this man's name happen to be Winter Rose?"

Carper's eyes widen.

"I've been around for a while."

He studies me, tapping his fingers against the piano keys. A gentle sound fills the air. "You see my dilemma?"

Glancing toward Alexis, I lean in even closer to Carper. "What if I told you the secret ingredient?"

"That's information you can't possibly have," he mutters.

"Try me."

"What do you know?"

More than I should. "You were born in America. After your father abandoned you and your mother, she took you both to China, where she originated. You like expensive food and watch wrestling. Your first name is Calvin. I have yet to hear your middle name, but I'm sure it's something regal, like *Louis* or *Charles*."

"It's *Jide*. In Mandarin, it means *to remember*."

Okay, so maybe his middle name doesn't match his personality. In all fairness, *Pero* means *feather*, and I'm nothing like the lightweight, fluffy things covering the bodies of birds.

"So, you've done some homework," he says. "Nothing a little digging on Google wouldn't mention, except the expensive food and wrestling. Tell me about the *ingredient*."

Hearing a noise from the other room, I see Alexis closing her book. Before my chance passes, I look directly at Carper. "Pure blood."

Carper scrunches his face, then brightens as if he understands. "You don't mean...?"

"Yes, I do. The blood of three chosen Lesaries was prophesied."

"But you can't possibly believe a legend will happen."

An idea pops into my mind. It could save Mom's future as well as bring Sam and me together. "It will because the chosen are close friends of mine."

He leans forward on the edge of his seat. "How can I find them?"

"If I tell you, can you promise not to harm them in any way?"

"I promise. You've had lessons with me for a couple of years now. I can be trusted."

I bite my lip. "Do you understand what knowledge can lead to?"

"Power. Riches. Pride."

I nod. "This experiment, combined with your personality, gives you either empowerment to save the world, or destroy yourself."

"I won't let it hurt me." He bounces his knees.

Swallowing hard, I pause. With a second chance, Carper wouldn't ruin the chosen. Elohim's revelation will alter his life, resulting in happiness for us all. *For Mom.* So she can have a second chance.

"The chosen is me."

It's a lie. Yes, I *am* one of the chosen, but merely through my future marriage to Sam and the blood of our future child. Carper doesn't have to find out. Once he experiments on me, instead of Mom, and doesn't find anything, he'll give up, thinking I'm not the solution. We'll all be safe from the torture, and Carper will be happy as an established geneticist, or something equally cool involving science.

Carper bursts out in laughter.

A peek through the door reveals Alexis looking upward. I give a smile, which she returns before opening her book.

He stops laughing when I don't join. "You're serious."

I nod, controlling the urge to take it all back. This was a good lie, right? If he takes the bait, I'll be helping my family. We'll all be better off.

"This is huge." He stands up with enthusiasm. "Try the harp. Maybe you're the one to make it play."

I have no desire to be anyone special anymore, but to please his curiosity, I approach the harp and pluck a string. It doesn't make a sound. Fine with me. If I was Carper's chosen *and* king (or queen, perhaps), I'd have major issues. More than I already have.

Carper shrugs. "I'll keep it around, anyway." He paces. "If I can utilize my studies without being caught, no one will be griping about me having taken it. Instead, they'll be thanking me for making the world a better place. Your mom doesn't have to know. We can continue doing music lessons, which will really be the experiments."

I'd forgotten he'd be stealing, according to U.S. law. Maybe I didn't consider this enough. Even if the material did belong to him, taking it from someone else posed a threat to his future and mine if he ever mentioned I was part of it. Plus, I'd be lying to Alexis.

"Thank you, Ruth." Carper extends a hand, and I numbly shake it. "Your information and participation will save millions of lives."

Nausea travels through my belly. What have I done?

23

DOUBT

SAM

A cloud carried me to a castle in the sky. I have no clue where I am, but I don't like it. Nothing this beautiful can be good, unless it's heaven itself, which I doubt. Stepping up the gold staircase and to the entrance, I shiver. Did whoever lives here welcome Pero?

Inside, a statue of an arrogant-looking man dressed in a tailored suit stands in the middle of an oval-shaped space. A brick wall holds three doors. Apartments, perhaps? Not likely in a castle. I climb the spiral staircase on my left, inspecting my options before proceeding. An exit sign marks a door at the top of the stairs, a helpful escape route if necessary. Of course, entering the unknown could be worse than an empty castle.

I scratch my neck. *What next?* Something falls and lands at my feet. I bend down to examine the dark material and pick up a piece of wood, its surface smooth. The color is familiar. It's a piece of Pero's necklace!

Pulling at the cords draped around my neck, I lift Pero's pendant. A tiny piece chipped off the feather's end. As I rub the surface, slivers of wood fall away. The dissolving pendant implies a parallel reality called *what if*. In this state, our minds are drawn in, though the body resists. This invitation is most commonly extended when everything is restored. For example, Henry returned Pero's heart, which is good but directly followed by opposition. If the devil can persuade one's mind that it's not satisfied, that person is deceived into following an idea or past that appears sexier but isn't. I've learned this from experience.

The *what if* state blurs reality, prompting the mind to consider different actions, which can reshape the future. Pero's changing history, which in turn is removing the prophecy involving our future descendants as part of the chosen three. If I don't stop her, I'll lose her, possibly forever.

"Damn the deceiver and his filthy lies!" I run down the spiral stairs, not caring that entering these rooms will risk my own sanity as well. When confronting the past, will I become dissatisfied as I did when in *what if* before? What happens if we're both removed from the prophecy?

Elohim, protect me with your armor. I'm entering the enemy's territory, yet Elohim's power cannot be shaken. In Him, I triumph.

I repeatedly knock on the door labeled with a number one. *What am I thinking?* Manners aren't necessary in a place like this. Ready to fight for the woman I love, I yank open the door, barge in, and slam it closed. I don't anticipate my father's surprised expression when he stands before me.

Stop right there, Sam. Breathe.

Pero won't be in this memory, so why bring me here unless to distract me from my mission? Make me give in for another chance to save him. Pero has to be in another room.

Yet, this is Dad—Salmon Abram—as real as the skin on my bones and the breath in my lungs. It won't hurt to say *hello*, for a moment.

"Did your mother get you all riled up?" He sets a hand on his hip, while the other grips an ax.

"What?" I glance behind me to find the scenery has completely changed. Instead of a door leading out of the room, I'm near a cabin, the same one my family lived in before moving to Green Meadow. Before Jimmy's father got into a fight with mine. Before Jimmy accidentally shot Salmon.

Somehow with Dad here, it feels perfect, like this was the home where I was meant to stay. Dad built the cabin with his own two hands. This is where he met and fell in love with Bahar. Where I initially encountered Ruth as a baby and then as a teen. The cabin is special.

Home.

"Chop some wood with me, will ya?" Dad places a block on a stump, then hands me the ax. "No better way to burn off some steam."

I'm in a meadow next to my family's cabin, chopping wood with my dad. It's surreal. I rest one foot on the stump, letting the hatchet hang by my side. Can I hug him? Re-acquaint myself with his smell, tuck it inside my mind to last another ten years.

"Something the matter, son?"

"Yeah." My eyes water. It's been a while since I cried, particularly for the man who's moved to another layer in my memories. Not forgotten, but not aching quite as intensely. "Why must we hurt so much?"

"Inner pain's a good thing," he says. "It means you care."

I set down the ax. "How would you respond if you lost someone you loved?"

He stays quiet, as if waiting for the right words. "Follow me." Dad nudges his head, then strolls toward the woods. A walk through the forest is Dad's happy place.

Catching up to him, I match his casual pace. I breathe in the scent of firs and pines, the wild mushrooms sprouting in moist soil. This is the smell that reminds me of Dad, living things.

"How long have these trees been around?" Dad lifts his gaze to the treetops.

"I don't know. Hundreds of years."

"How many generations of people have they seen live and die?"

"Maybe dozens."

"Do the trees still grow?"

"Of course."

"Why do you think that is?"

"Because loggers haven't cut them down. And the sun and rain keep them alive."

"Wrong." He stops, then turns to face me. "Their roots keep them alive. If roots aren't established deep under the ground, the trees will lose their core strength and die. You understand?"

I nod. "As I'm rooted in Elohim, the storms in life won't kill me. Even when things hurt, I'll keep getting stronger as I grow from my establishment in Him."

He places a hand on my shoulder. It lands like an easy weight to carry, as if he recognizes the strength in me and calls it out.

Stand taller like a tree.

Grow.

Ground yourself deeper still.

A hand still on my shoulder, he closes his eyes. Although he doesn't speak out loud, I feel Elohim's power through Dad's prayer. A surge courses through my blood, preparing me for the battle ahead. A gentle presence settles in, quieting my grieving soul.

I am well.

Dad opens his eyes and wraps his arms around me. His hugs were always comforting, never a brief pat on the arm, but rather a deep embrace with a tight squeeze. As a boy, I used to squirm under his hold, ready to go play. At this moment, with my face against his shoulder and tears dampening his shirt, I embrace him back, delaying the inevitable moment when I must let go.

A bell chimes from the distance, and Dad pulls back. "Dinner's ready. You better get going."

"Walk with me?" I ask.

I'll never see him again, and I'm not ready. I could change the future. All it would require is staying away from the property in Green Meadow. Then the accident wouldn't happen, Dad wouldn't die, and we'd figure out a way to escape before Jimmy's dad hurts us.

I clear my thoughts. It's a lie. If Dad doesn't die from a gun, he'll go another way.

Dad shakes his head. "Some paths are best traveled alone."

"Why?"

"Space allows the mind to think and pray, helps me become a better father and husband. My love for your mom grows when I've had some solitude."

Some, not permanent. I can't tell him death is around the corner. I can't save his life any more than I can save Pero's. Their fates are out of my control. Yet I will stay rooted and won't change the past. For a while longer, I'll heed Dad's advice and walk alone.

"I love you, Dad." I turn to leave.

"Love you, too, Sam," he calls. "You make me proud."

I glimpse back, treasuring years spent within the protection and guidance of this profound father. He continues walking, his steps determined and strong. I want to be like him for Pero and my future children. They will have many years of my love, grace, and gratitude because I will be rooted in my true source of power, Elohim.

Nearing the front door of the cabin, I break into a wide smile. Beyond that door is my future bride. My Ruth.

I choose to accept the pain and move forward. I'd do it all

over again for her. Dad's right. Solitude does wonders for a man in love.

As I step over the threshold—which will direct me toward the castle—I hear Pero calling my name. Then, I spot her.

Yet I've passed, unable to return.

She's gone.

24

ESCAPE

PERO

I am at the cabin. From the castle in the sky, the door labeled *two* brought me to this familiar sanctuary, but since I'd been Carper's experiment in replace of Mom, who lives at the cabin now?

The weight of what I thought was a good idea nags me. Carper could've still become conceited and driven toward power from my influence. I may have solved nothing, or maybe I made things much worse.

I'm standing in the field behind the cabin. The sun is bright, the atmosphere calm. I don't see anyone around. What if the house was abandoned? What a shame it would be for no one to occupy such a beautiful place.

As I near the edge, I smell a freshly cooked meal and hear a bell ring, making me jump and clutch my chest. Someone's here. Creeping my way toward the front of the house, I crouch beneath an open window when a voice calls.

"Dinner's ready!"

The woman sounds a whole lot like Mom. If it is, at least Bahar's safe and forever happy with her husband, Salmon, and their son, Sam.

I pause before peeking over the edge of the window frame. The kitchen counter holds a steaming skillet with heaps of potatoes, greens, and meat. The smell of rosemary and garlic intoxicates my senses. A flash of long black hair and light brown skin moves past the counter. I duck before getting a good look at her. The parts of her I saw gives me sign enough that it's who I suspected.

Mom's dinner announcement must mean I'm back in time to when she lived with her first husband, Salmon. If Sam's been born, I might get to see him. The question is, at what age? It would be fun to find Sam as a cute kid or teen. Was he gentle and sweet at seven, or did he often get into trouble?

Finding out whether Sam is five or fifteen first requires a step inside. Chances are, Mom won't recognize me because she will have only known herself as Sam's mom, while I would've grown up as Alexis's daughter. Sam won't remember me either, but perhaps I'll have the chance to "meet" him again, and the second he lays eyes on me, his ten-year-old self will recognize I'm the one he'll marry someday. Then I'll have to return to Earth so Sam can grow up, and everything will return to normal. I hope.

Gathering courage, I scurry to the front of the house, then pause when I see the front doorknob turning.

"Sam!" I call out.

He turns his head, recognition on his face, but he's already stepped through the doorway. When he doesn't rush to me, I run around the porch, climb up the steps, and barge inside the cabin.

Sam's gone, but Mom stops mid-stride, a stack of plates in hand, eyes fastened on me.

"Hi." What do you say when you're in the same room as the woman you've always referred to as *mom*, yet you're unsure if she remembers you or not? "You rang for dinner?"

She hesitates, then places the stack of plates on the counter and smiles. "I wasn't expecting people outside of my family to answer the call. Of course, you're welcome to join us. It'll be me, my husband, and son. Not very exciting company, I'm afraid. My name's Bahar Abram. Are you a friend of Sam's?"

"Yes." Well, it remains true, even if he's four-years-old. "My name is Ruth. Are you familiar with the name Alexis Nesim?"

"I am. We were friends roughly twenty years ago and reacquainted after she returned to Origo. Poor thing's been through a lot."

Alexis must've left Origo to live on Earth, then returned. But why? "Alexis is my mother."

Technically, my last name would've been Nesim if I had grown up with my birth mother, Alexis, and Sam's last name would've been Abram if he had grown up with Bahar. My last name is now Moshe because Matthew adopted me. However, my birth father would have given me the last name Carper. Is my life confusing, or what? For Mom's sake, I'll assume our original names are the current ones, since, you know, I may have changed history.

"I know who you are!" she exclaims.

"You do?"

"You're the talk of the town since Alexis returned. When did you arrive?"

"A couple minutes ago."

"Have a seat, honey." Mom leads me to the square table and motions to a chair.

Taking it, I wonder at the excitement in her tone. I cringe, hoping I'm not famous for escaping prison after lying to Carper and Alexis.

Mom grabs a plate and fills it with two scoops of stew, placing it in front of me. "I bet you're starving." She sits next to me and watches.

Food is the last thing on my mind, yet I eat to make her happy. The stew is warm and satisfying, even if a bit too salty.

Mom waits until I've taken a couple of bites before speaking. "As soon as Sam returns, I'll ask him to get Alexis. Your mom will be the happiest woman alive."

"You think so?" By keeping her talking, maybe she'll answer the mystery of how she knows me.

"Of course! You've been missing for two years on Earth."

"Right. It's already been two years. That was fast."

When Mom rubs her chin and grimaces, I realize I may not have given the appropriate response about someone who's been missing.

"How else do you know me?" I stuff another spoonful of stew to keep me quiet.

"Well, I've heard the stories. How they think you ended up in China. That Alexis dropped you off for music lessons one day, and you and your music teacher never returned."

I raise my brows, slowly chewing the last bits of food in my mouth before swallowing.

"I'm sorry to bring up such a sensitive topic. We don't have to talk at all until your mom arrives."

"No, tell me more." So, I *did* replace Mom as Carper's experiment, which means I'm returning from Carper's hidden lab in the Forbidden City. It didn't make any difference, except keeping Mom away from Carper. I didn't carry the right blood type to save worlds.

"I think you've been through enough without me blabbing." She stands and approaches a window, peers out. "They should be here by now."

"I thought I saw Sam come into the house right before me."

She shakes her head, squinting through the glass. "No one enters this tiny place without being seen."

Strange. Maybe when Sam entered, he landed somewhere else.

Mom walks toward the front door. "I'd better check. If I can't find them, I'll take you to Alexis myself."

I stand. "I'll go with you."

"If you're up to it."

"I am."

We exit the cabin and head toward the woods.

"They often go for walks before dinner." Mom's voice carries worry.

"I'm sure we'll find them." Well, I'm sure we'll find Salmon. I doubt Sam's here since I apparently watched his ghost enter the home not too long ago.

"How did you meet Sam?"

I perk up at the mention of him. "It's complicated."

Mom gives me a sideways glance. "You're the one he's always talking about."

"What does he say about me?"

"Oh, stuff. How you are the only other Lesarien around his age with a wood carving hobby."

I snort. "Definitely not me."

"Oops. Too bad. You seem nice, but I liked that other mysterious girl."

Ugh. How is Sam supposed to fall in love with me again if he's got a crush on some wood-carving shorty? If we don't marry, then changing history will have been for nothing. At least he's not a toddler.

I'm relieved when Mom doesn't press about my friendship with Sam. Everything will be straightened out soon, I'm sure.

When we're nearer to the woods, a figure runs toward us through the trees. My hand blocks the setting sun to see better.

Sam!

I resist the urge to run up to him. What if he doesn't remember me? I am in *his* world after having changed his past life.

When Mom gains speed, I follow.

"What's wrong?" she asks.

Sam's out of breath. He does a double take in my direction, seeming to wonder who I am, then focuses on Mom. "It's—"

A baby's cry interrupts him.

I lift my head and strain my ear. "Where's that cry coming from?"

I step into the woods.

"Don't go in there." Sam pulls on my arm. "It's not safe in the woods."

He's said this before.

"Right here." Mom walks a few feet into the woods. At a tree's base is a baby.

It can't be! The story changed. Were Elohim's plans unstoppable? Mom's reason for finding me as a baby remains unclear, yet it's unfolding, despite events being turned up-side-down. I won't stop it. Bahar will find me. It's settled.

The baby's wrapped tightly in a blanket, flailing her arms, searching for someone to carry her. I see familiar traits, mirroring the first time I saw myself lying in the forest. No doubt, it's me.

As Mom reaches into the hollow of a tree and picks up the baby, Alexis enters the scene, crying out and rushing toward us. "My Ruth! My Ruth!"

Mom points to grown-up me. "We found her!"

But Alexis's gaze is fixed on the baby. "How did Ruth end up there?"

Mom cocks one eyebrow, her head tilted as she looks at me. At that moment, the tree behind Mom opens into a doorway, light spilling.

Alexis halts. "Nooo!" I hear the rush of her feet against the tall grass.

"Behind you!" Sam nearly knocks me over as he charges forward. He trips over a root, spilling to the floor. With a sharp intake of breath, he jerks away from the ground, holding onto his cheek. Blood streaks in a thin line across his face. I recall, then, what he said to me once, how he'd fallen and cut his cheek right before his mom disappeared before his eyes. The scar formed later, but he seems to dismiss the pain, fixated on Mom and the baby in her arms, about to be enveloped by moss and bark.

"Stop!"

But his warning isn't enough.

With the baby close to her heart, Mom turns. The tree swallows them whole.

I've rehearsed this scene before. Alexis stomping toward me in a fury. Me stepping back. Sam holding onto Alexis's shirt, then locking her in his strong arms.

Next, Alexis will scream at me.

"What'd you do with Ruth!" As predicted, she shouts in my face, spit flying like sparks from her mouth.

I don't defend myself like I did before, and still she chokes on a sob, crumbles to the ground, and tucks her head low.

Again, pain settles in Sam's eyes.

"I'm sorry." I think I said those same words as they roll off my tongue with ease.

This isn't a rehearsal. This is life on repeat.

Sam stammers, glancing between the two of us strangers. Tears gather in his eyes. "I...I'm sorry. My dad...it's bad."

That's not in the script.

Sam leaves us, weaving around trees and leaping over branches. I've never seen him move so fast. Something's seriously wrong. Alexis doesn't leave her curled up position, unaware her twenty-two-year-old *Ruth* stands right in front of her.

Not wanting Sam to deal with an emergency on his own, I leave Alexis behind. It doesn't take long to catch up with Sam, then pass him.

I'm the first to find Salmon lying on the ground and unresponsive.

No!

He's not supposed to get hurt. I changed the outcome, becoming the sacrifice for the ones I love! I can't bear the thought of Sam losing his parents again. He rarely mentions it, but I'm familiar with the signs of suffering.

Kneeling, I place two fingers against Salmon's neck, feeling for any sign of life. Nothing. CPR class was a requirement in high school, but can I remember? I center my two palms on his chest, shoulders directly over hands, elbows locked. Do I compress one inch down or two? I perform something in-between.

No breath.

Come on!

Another round, then I release.

When Sam approaches, I look up at him, his form blurry through my clouded eyes.

"I tried." My voice cracks. "I can't do anything else."

"It's too late." He drops next to Salmon.

This isn't fair! Sam's life offered a fresh start. He had his mom and dad. I lied to Carper about me carrying the prophesied blood in order to make Sam and Bahar's dreams come true, simply to see the same outcome. It wasn't Jimmy's gun that killed Salmon, but an alternate death wouldn't diminish Sam's grief.

Why, Elohim!

My power is made great in your weakness.

I get that, Elohim, but can't your power make Salmon live?

His meaning hits me like being plunged into icy water. By taking matters into my own hands—changing history to make an outcome I think is best—I'm saying I possess enough power to control the future.

I don't.

Only Elohim can prevent death or give life. How dare I challenge His power! If He's good, then He can hold the most fragile of beings. If He's King, then His power dwells *in* us, even through the darkest of shadows.

Dropping my head into my hands, I weep. *Forgive me, Elohim. I tried to take control, and bad things still happened. Hold on to me because I can't carry anything without it slipping from my grasp.*

A light but firm pressure presses against my upper back. "I've never met you, Miss." Sam's calming voice puts a rest to my tears. "I'm not as good of a hugger as my dad, but I'll try my best if you could use one."

What a compassionate heart, that he would comfort a stranger while grieving his father. I nod, as he helps me to my feet and brings me in. Salmon must've been one great hugger. Sam's embrace is tight but not too tight. Never a hint of impatience or hurry. Giving space for me to leave when I'm ready. The steady beating of his heart, the woodsy smell against his shoulder, the strength of his embrace—tight but not too tight and so beautifully familiar—bring a flood of rest.

"Thank you," I whisper.

When I release, Sam steps back as if feeling awkward after he'd suggested the idea.

Then I remember. He doesn't know me.

A wall rises around my heart, a dose of sadness drowning the brief peace I felt once upon a hug. I no longer belong with him. I'm alone, desperate to find the Sam who waits for me to return into his arms and never let go. But it is impossible to recall a past that never happened, and I've ruined all hope of a second chance.

"Sam, I'm sorry for your loss."

The angry, grief-filled memories I tried to save are buried in history, but so is the man I love. Turning, I take off into the woods, leaving him behind.

25

LOVE

PERO

The ache in my chest tightens. If only I could leave this blasted memory and return to the present. I get the point. Open doors make life complicated. Then again, why do I always have the urge to go through them?

When I've reached the part of the woods where Sam first met me, I stop. Will he return to me, or is it too late for another chance? I've made a mess of things, have turned to Sam for help far too often.

Yet minutes later, I hear feet shuffling. I gulp down the fear that he won't want me this time around and step into the moonlight. He navigates the dark with ease and purpose.

When he's close enough for me to see the white of his eyes and the cut along his cheek, he stops. "Who are you?"

"Your chosen."

He scans me, his brow furrowed in focus. "I believe you."

As soon as the words are out of his mouth, I remember him having spoken them before.

"Have we met in the past?" In the dim lighting, I notice his blush.

"Yes."

He studies my face, as if determined to figure me out by finding the right freckle. "What's your name?"

"Ruth."

"Ruth," he repeats. "Same name as the baby who disappeared with my mom."

I nod. "Same name, same person."

His gaze doesn't flicker. "How does that work?"

I shrug. "It just does."

I pause, sensing questions resting on the tip of his tongue. Then I wait more, until my longing for whatever he'll say grows stronger than the agonizing silence.

Stumbling for the right words, he finally speaks. "Why'd you respond the way you did when my dad...?" He shuffles his feet. "Did you know him well?"

Tears resurface when I remember Salmon's body lying at rest. "I was grieving for you."

"But why?"

"You look so much like him. He was handsome, a beautiful person. My mom...I mean, your mom loved him deeply. You did, too. Both of them." I shake my head. "I couldn't save them."

"It wasn't your job."

I sniffle, then attempt a weak smile. "Elohim told me a similar thing."

He jolts and scans the forest, eyes wide.

"Are we in danger?" I ask.

"No." When his eyes return to mine, his gaze shifts, lingering longer, exploring more deeply. "Why are you here?"

Good question. At first, I was driven through the castle by a desire to fix the past. Now all I want is to marry the man who's reclaimed my heart. "Looking for you."

He swallows hard, taking a couple of steps closer. Placing a hand on my jaw, his thumb makes tiny circles. His gaze lingers on my lips. "You found me."

I suck in a breath, leaning into his touch. Then, I notice his cheek, the cut completely clear. I graze my fingers against the surface, the stubble across his face sending chills down my spine.

"It's gone, isn't it?" He leans in further.

I nod, my throat closing off.

"Ruth." This time my name is not laced in curiosity; it is imploring. Like a prayer. Like the light of dawn proclaiming a secret garden long abandoned. "I know who you are."

"And who am I, Sam?"

The air between us throbs with heat. I'm drowning in his closeness, anticipating his next move.

"My Ruth."

The hum of my name sends flutters in my belly. He remembers me. He wants me.

When his lips are an inch from mine, he whispers, "May I?"

"Yeah," I say, my tone a thick murmur.

He closes the gap between us and kisses me.

The initial contact feels like an explosion of passion. I tremble, drinking of his dark features, like being bathed in the most beautiful of living things. His arms encircle my waist, and my hands wrap around his neck, drawing him nearer. As he deepens the kiss, sparks shoot throughout my whole body. The intensity I'd previously felt with each look and touch was nothing compared to this overpowering encounter. When I think I'll never come up for air, he tapers off, leaving me breathless and empty.

"You're incredible." His face brightens, a wide smile spreading. "Please don't say I'm dreaming, because that was way too good. I can't believe I waited so long to kiss you."

I blink in surprise. "So, you *do* remember me."

"Every bit. I'm back to the present."

I give him a mischievous grin. "What's the name my parents gave me?"

"Pero."

"Who are my biological parents?"

"Alexis and Carper, but not from the typical way babies are made."

"Thank Elohim! That would've been weird in every way."

Sam laughs.

"Last question," I say.

"Ready."

"Do you recall our first kiss?"

"Are you kidding me?" He almost staggers back. "I woke up to whatever magic spell you had me under."

"I agree it was more than amazing, but what do you mean?"

"I've been trying to find you. I followed you through the open door in your bedroom closet and ended up in a sky castle. The first door in the castle led me to a walk with my dad. The second door brought me to you in this exact spot, right before I asked what you were doing here."

I punch him playfully. "What happened to our boundaries?"

"I'm planning on marrying you as soon as we're out of here."

"What about Henry?"

"It's all taken care of." As if receiving a gold medal at the Olympics, he lifts the chain from around his neck and holds up the feather pendant proudly.

I look closer. "I see one."

His smile dissipates as he glances down and feels around his neck for the other chain. "I hope I didn't drop it." He checks his pockets and shakes out his shirt and pants.

"We'll find it."

"We have to. That necklace has been passed down for centuries."

"Before we search for it...." I hesitate, wanting to be sensitive to the big event that just happened right before the other big event that just happened. "Do you still grieve the loss of your parents?"

He sighs. "Was that the memory you revisited?"

I nod, a knot in my throat preventing me from speaking.

He brings a thumb to my hair, tucks a strand behind my ear. "The wound hasn't healed, but Elohim's been faithful to bring me peace."

A tear trails down my cheek. "I was there when it happened. I tried to fix the past by becoming Carper's experiment, but it didn't work. If Bahar hadn't picked me up as a baby, I would have reached your dad before he...."

"It wasn't your fault, Ruth." He takes my face in his hands and looks directly into my eyes. "Never think you caused this. It's not in our power to prevent bad things from happening to good people."

He kisses me tenderly, then releases. "Enough of the woods' depressing memories. What do you say we search the castle for the necklace?"

"Great idea, but how do we get out of here?"

He nods in the direction behind me. "Turn around."

A tree with an exit waits for us.

Every so often, an answer is right behind the question. Other times, it's after a kiss.

26

RESCUE

PERO

The necklace is missing from the castle, but a slightly open third door hints at someone inside.

"It's got to be there." I peek through the crack. Darkness. "Maybe someone found it and walked inside to find the owner."

Sam folds his arms. "Or stole it."

I shrug. "I'm kind of intrigued."

"Have you ever heard the proverb, curiosity killed the cat?"

I snicker. "Like I wrote in my letter to you, I'm not a cat."

"So you don't have nine lives in case this kills you?"

"Where's your sense of adventure?" I grab onto Sam's hand and pull him toward the door while walking backward. "Besides, we need to find the necklace."

He yanks me toward him and keeps me near his chest. "It's not safe, Pero."

I let myself sink into his embrace. He's right, of course. Hasn't my drive for exploration harmed enough? You'd think I would've learned my lesson by now. "Okay, Mr. Nesim. Let's get out of here."

He lifts my chin, his gaze dipping to my lips. "Not yet."

I lean in toward him when a loud crash sounds from through door three, causing us to jump back.

"What was that?" I tip-toe up to the door.

"Careful," Sam says from behind me. "You can't trust anything from this universe."

"Where are we, anyway?"

"It's kind of like a stream of consciousness called *what if*. Basically, deception comes in sneaky forms, making you believe if the past could be changed, you'll have ultimate control of your future."

"Huh." Sounds familiar. "That explains a lot."

"Now do you understand why we shouldn't be here?" he asks.

I nod. "I'd rather not make another drastic mistake."

"That, and the necklaces are slowly disintegrating. The longer we're in here, the more we'll lose our desire for Elohim."

"Great," I say. "Another reason to find my necklace."

From inside room three, a scream pierces the air.

I startle. "Someone's calling for help!"

As I take another step forward, Sam pulls me back. "Part of the Deceiver's work is to make you believe something's wrong."

"But what if it is real?"

Sam seems to be thinking through.

Another scream.

"Okay. I suppose it'd be worth seeing if the necklace is in there." He doesn't seem too happy about it. "But if anything feels off or one of us starts causing a different outcome from our past, we leave."

"You have my word."

As if hurrying before he changes his mind, Sam jerks the door open, grabs my hand, then brings me into the darkness.

Inside, I'm sitting in bed in a room at night. Where am I?

"Sam?"

No one responds.

Dragging my feet over the edge, I feel my way toward a counter, my eyes slowly adjusting to the dark. "Is anyone here?"

Silence answers.

Was the scream a trick to lure us inside? If so, it worked. And now the screamer and Sam are missing. *Great.* We should've left while we had the chance.

Objects like shadows surround me: a mini fridge, an open room with a bathroom sink, and a large piece of furniture. I inch my way closer and feel it with my hands. A wardrobe.

I'm in Mom's old room in Moon City! More like the suite version of a prison cell.

A loud thud echoes through the ceiling. The last time I was here, the same thing happened right before I went up to investigate. I'd had a nightmare about Carper and woken up, which means the screams we heard were my own. Sam's not in the same room with me because he's in the greenhouse...with Henry. The necklace has to be there too! I'd buried it in the soil of one of the garden beds.

I pull down the ladder from the ceiling and climb. The rail underneath my hands vibrates from another thud above me. *Yep. Here we go again.*

Unlike the last occasion, I don't hesitate to climb up the stairs. The sooner I can get to Sam, the better. He should recognize me now; we came in here together.

"I heard something," I hear Sam say. "Maybe she's coming up from her room."

Does Sam remember having said those exact words before? Or does reliving the past cause repetition without control?

"Don't scare her," Henry's voice says.

I pause at the top of the stairs, grinning as I listen to their dialogue. It's like watching a good movie you haven't seen in years, familiar and just as enjoyable.

"She shouldn't be surprised," Sam says.

"Yeah, but she had no idea when we'd come, and we still need to find her daughter."

Ha! The woman they'd been looking for was Mom. I was the daughter.

"You mean the pretty Pero." Sam again. Is that a jealous tone? I missed that before. This is a good reason repeating history is worthwhile. You get a fresh perspective.

"I never said she was pretty."

Sure, Henry.

A chuckle from Sam. "You didn't have to."

That's my cue.

I step onto the roof, bracing myself for Henry's exuberant reaction.

"Pero!" Henry runs to me, spins me in a circle, then sets me down.

Even though I was prepared, I can't help smiling at my old friend. Did he look *that* young? Bouncy curls, smooth baby face, bright blue eyes. A classic teen heart-throbber.

I skip the original dialogue we'd exchanged about how it appeared Henry had sold me to Carper. We're past that since he's returned the heart he stole from inside me.

I tilt my head toward Sam, addressing Henry. "Who's your friend?" I grin even wider. This is so much fun! If we ever get out of this castle, I should pursue acting.

Sam steps closer, his course black hair flipped in the front like a small wave. The same stubble beard shadows his jawline, but without a scar.

His eyes shine in the moonlight's reflection from behind me. My lingering gaze isn't merely a memorized part. If Henry wasn't aware we technically just met, I'd run up to Sam and kiss him hard enough to make Cathena squirm. Cathena told me she'd spied on us during this encounter, that it was obvious how drawn we were to each other at first sight. I resist finding young Cathena—then named Stone—through the glass wall separating our greenhouses.

Besides, who would want to look away at a moment like this?

Sam

We're in Moon City. I haven't had a chance to tell Pero this is my third experience with this memory on the rooftop. Well, technically second, but it's the third time this scenario has been replayed. The first was when Salmon and another Lesarien man spied on the land. A woman hid them on her roof behind bundles of flax. Her name was Rahab, a prostitute. Dad helped rescue her before the city crumbled, and she joined the Lesaries. Dad's love redeemed her past.

A year later, they had me and settled in, but life became hard with wars, forcing us to leave the comfort of our cabin and join the Lesaries in battles. Searching for an escape from the war, my family moved to Earth and stayed in a small town in the U.S. called Green Meadow. We worked on a farm to live there. When Dad died from an accident on the farm, Mom and I returned to Origo.

Years later, when the opportunity came for Mom to enter *what if*, she jumped at the chance to change her past, hoping it would save her husband and remove the label of being a prostitute. She became Bahar, which is *Rahab* spelled backwards and means *spring*, like the season. Bahar had changed, and as a result, so did our lives.

Given a second chance, she ran away from her prison in the Forbidden City and met Dad in a cabin in Origo. They fell in love again, got married, had me, and lived happily ever after.

Until one day she picked up a baby from under a tree, proving destiny never can be changed.

As much as I wish to bring back Dad, I'm glad Mom's future included that baby. Because without Pero, my destiny wouldn't have been so beautiful.

27

KILL

SAM

I've met Pero before in the greenhouse, but the way she's looking at me now makes it feel like our first meeting. I feel a slight blush on my cheeks as I mirror her fixed stare.

"This is Sam," Henry says. "Sam, this is Pero."

"Henry told me about you." I study the floor, then peek up to find her hiding laughter.

"I've heard about you, too."

Oh, she's loving this. I give her a wink.

She nods her head toward the ladder. "Let's go inside before anyone sees us."

After we settle around the kitchenette, Pero offers us drinks as she opens the fridge door. I can't see her face, but I can tell her cough is covering more giggles.

Perhaps she's going through the motions to have fun reliving a good memory. While I'm also enjoying myself, I'm also realizing we need to relive each interaction leading up to where the necklace must be hidden in the garden bed above us. Then we'll pray for an exit before things worsen.

Pero sets three drinks in front of us, which we don't touch, then sits at the bar stool Henry pulls out for her.

"Why were you looking for my mom?" she asks.

"We met your mom here a few months ago," Henry says. "Bahar recognized we weren't from Moon City and took us in. She said she would tie a red scarf to a window for us to find her. Is your mom okay?"

I've been so absorbed in my and Pero's little game, I forgot Henry is living in this scene as if it's the first time, which means his feelings for Pero are still fresh. I must take this seriously if we are to find the necklace and escape before we're tempted to change the past.

"She can't come with us because Carper took her," Pero says, "but I think this scarf means she'd want me to go with you."

"I can try to find her." Henry's voice sounds eager, like he's been waiting for the right moment to win Pero's affection.

She shakes her head. "My mom asked for me to hide, and nothing can be done at this point. Guards are all over Moon City." She steals another look at me and lands there. Crossing her leg over the other, she places her hand on her chin, an adorable smirk on her face. "So, Sam, you seem to be the man with a plan. Do you have a map to show us the way out?"

I mimic her, resting chin to hand and wiggling my brows. "I have an idea."

"Good, because I just got lost in your eyes."

Henry's jaw drops.

I burst out laughing. She may not have intentionally flirted the first time she did that cute little thing, but she definitely knows what she's doing now. Top priority: find that necklace. Henry may shut himself off completely from her if she contin-ues, and I'd rather not find out how that might affect our future.

From the roof, Pero tucks her hand into her pocket, then

pulls out a tight fist. "I'll hide this so Carper doesn't track me." She kneels in front of the soil, hiding where she's searching for the necklace. Looks like she also figured out where it would be.

I peer over her shoulder, spotting the pendant lying on the dirt. The chip is still evident, the whole necklace more worn and thin than before.

It is good to live in unity.

I jolt, curious why Elohim would speak to me now when we're reliving in the past. The pendant against my chest becomes warmer. I balance it in my palm. *What do you mean by that, Elohim?*

Don't let anyone separate what I've joined.

Pero and I will work in unity. Maybe bringing the necklaces together symbolizes what He wants to do with us, together.

Leaning in, I whisper. "Wear it, but don't let Henry see."

"What are you two whispering about?" Henry is suspicious, but we should be able to move fast enough to avoid altering the past.

"Only helping Pero hide the necklace."

With both hands on the sides of her head, she mimics a stretch as she brings the chain over her neck.

"It's warm," she says in a hushed tone.

"Don't move. Follow my lead."

"Seems like you could use some help." Henry walks toward us.

"Almost done," I call to him. Moving closer to Pero's side, I bring my feather pendant forward and match it against hers. A light flashes across the sky. Pero's pendant shows no more signs of chipping or faded wood. Joining our necklaces seems to have restored whatever history we made a mess of.

"Was that lightning?" Henry scans the sky through the glass ceiling.

The next moment, Moon City disappears faster than a blink. Pero and I appear inside the castle.

Except it's no longer empty.

I should've guessed a statue in a world like this wouldn't stay still. The statue who stood in the middle of the foyer is the same man before us. He wears a tailored suit, hair held in a bun at the base of his neck. I've never cared for man buns. A lazy, hipster style, in my opinion. Red flags alarm my senses as he ambles in our direction with an unnerving smile.

I clasp on to Pero's trembling hand. We've become like statues, evaluating the situation, sniffing for threats, eyeing the winding staircase leading up to the exit.

"Sam and Pero, the inseparable pair." The man grins as if he made a joke. "Welcome to my castle."

I won't laugh that he somehow knows our names and is the owner of this wretched place. We missed our chance to leave, but then, the necklace.

"Who are you?" My voice carries more confidence than I feel inside.

He keeps on smiling. "I think you know."

"Deceiver."

"Call me Rife."

Rife sounds like *knife*. I don't like knives unless they're used to carve things.

When he extends a hand toward mine, I don't accept it. Stepping in front of Pero, I let out a low growl. "We were just leaving."

He frowns. "I wouldn't do that."

"I won't let you decide what we do or don't do. Now, if you'll excuse us." I lead Pero around Rife, reaching the stairs.

"It's too late, Sam," he calls. "Your past is ruined."

Is he aware the feathers have been restored? The past should be the way it was before. "I don't think so." I pull Pero forward and up the stairs, noticing her unusual quietness, eyes wide like a deer in the headlights.

"I'm not talking about the restored necklaces in Room 3."

I ignore him. The sooner we leave, the better.

"Is she aware her story isn't true?" Rife asks.

"What's he talking about?" Pero's voice shakes.

"Don't listen to him. He's a liar."

"You're right." Rife's arms fold. "I suppose it's no big deal that the woman you love killed your father."

"Sam?" Her voice is forced, anxious.

"Not now, Ruth." We reach the top of the stairs. I can't open the door fast enough.

As I turn the handle, Rife calls out. "Are you sure about going that way?"

I hesitate, debating whether to believe him. I finally decide it's better to discover what lays beyond this exit than to stay around. "Positive."

Pero holds on tight as I open the door and we walk in, leaving the devil behind.

28

LEARN

PERO

I am sitting at a bar in a little black dress. Next to me is the guy I danced with at Mr. Rose's party years ago. I escaped using him as a diversion from the guards. What was his name? Jasper? Jared? Well, that one guy is demanding the bartender make him a drink called the Bee's Knees.

A guard at Rose's party watches me. Should I run again? As a time traveler, discovery could mean trouble for my future. I groan. So much for the exit taking us to the present. At least we got away from Strife. I mean, Rife.

"A beautiful girl like you can't be too careful."

I gasp and swivel in my chair to find Sam. "You made it!"

He's styled his hair perfectly, as before, wearing dark jeans and a gray tailored jacket that makes his eyes appear a deeper brown. How can I make this be Sam's wardrobe every day?

"In a previous life, you were so scared, you wouldn't look at me." He takes my hand. Bringing it close to his lips, he gives it a quick kiss and winks. "I'm Sam."

I smile. "Nice to meet you, Sam. My name is Ruth."

He draws closer. "I about lost it when you first gave me your middle name at this same spot."

I lean in, as if preparing to hear a great secret. "Tell me more."

"I wondered if you were the same Ruth I'd lost long ago."

"Really?" I smile.

"I was so full of hope that I almost lost my composure," he says.

"What would've happened if you had?"

"Uncle Rose would've called my bluff and kicked me out."

"Kind of like he's trying to do now?"

Sam follows my gaze. Rose is coming toward us with a scowl on his face before he's stopped by a guest.

"Should we leave before they catch us?" Sam asks.

"Probably."

"How about a walk?" Sam asks. "The rose garden is in full bloom."

Standing, I adjust my dress, reminded of how uncomfortable it is to move in this thing. "Exactly what I had in mind."

I hook my arm through Sam's. "Your company is far better than Rife's."

"Never trust a man wearing a bun."

"I like man buns. They're sophisticated."

Sam grimaces. "I hope you're not disappointed when I don't grow my hair out."

"You with a man bun? It doesn't suit you."

"What a relief!"

"Hey!" *Jace.* That's the name of the Bee's Knees guy. "Where are you going?"

"Great to meet you, Jace. Thank you for saving me out there." I point to the dance floor.

"You sure you want to go with this guy? I'm no dew-dropper."

I nod. "See you."

"Absolutely." Jace frowns.

Sam and I walk past the dancers and library, heading for the hall.

"The word *absolutely* still sounds sad coming from that guy. I think you broke his heart." Sam pauses when Rose stands in our way. "Uncle Rose, great party."

Rose isn't really Sam's uncle, as he explained before. He's more like a distant cousin.

"Thank you." Rose tips his head. "I trust you are aware you're under surveillance."

"Yes, sir. I was about to show her the garden. Nothing more, sir."

Rose grunts, then leaves us alone.

Knowing full well what's coming, I brace myself as Sam pushes me. A maid swerves around me, the tray of food wobbling on her palm. The hall door leads to the laundry room. We enter, and similar to the past, Sam locks it behind him. It's helpful to be aware of the next move, which is why I'm not surprised when we hear someone trying to open the door.

"Pero?"

I groan. "Do we have to let Cherry in this time?"

"If we change the past, Cherry will never reunite with Jehoshua."

"Okay, say we let her in. How far do we go with this? If we stay around too long, I'll end up on a plane to China while you stay behind."

"Hello?" A knock on the door from Cherry. "I can hear you two talking in there."

"Let's find a way before you head for China. Here." He touches my pendant with his own. Nothing happens. He frowns. "Hmm. Remember when we took that walk in front of your dad's house before you left?"

"Of course."

"We should revisit our starting point to resolve this, at your old house."

"Perfect."

Before Sam turns the knob to let Cherry in, he gives me a full and slow body scan. "You do look exquisite."

A pounding sensation works its way up from my gut to my face. So, he *had* been controlling himself when he previously said those words without steering his gaze away from my face. Now, he purposely lets his eyes travel, desire written plainly on his face, proving he finds me attractive. Such self control when he didn't look at my body before! I swear, I love this man more every minute.

The next two hours run smoothly. Nothing in the memory changes or catches us by surprise. I'm much more patient with Cherry's outbursts of tears during the hour drive from Rose's place at the Oregon coast, all the way to the driveway of my old home in Green Meadow. Why fret over Cherry when things will be alright in the end? While it's nice to be assured of what's next in life, I'd be exhausted if this was my daily routine. Where's the joy in rehearsed living?

Elohim, we really could use a way out of here soon.

My walk with Sam doesn't come fast enough, yet here we are. Reliving another cherished memory.

"Hanging in there?" Sam interlaces his fingers with mine.

"I'm glad to be with you, but home sounds really nice right now."

"Back to the Lesaries in Origo or on the farm here?"

"Not sure. I'd feel at home wherever you are."

He kisses my hand.

I don't deserve such treatment. Not after I messed up the past. "I need to tell you about what happened while in *what if*."

"Don't forget we're still in it."

"Yes, and we should try not to alter the past any more. I'm already busted."

"Well," he says, "whatever you did, it gave me a moment with my dad before he died. That meant a lot to me."

"I'm so glad!" Yet, Sam needed to hear the truth of everything that had happened. I dive into the story, including every detail about me telling Carper I was the chosen and that he had experimented on me instead as a result. But Alexis still searched for me and Bahar and Sam stayed to help. If they hadn't been so focused on helping Alexis and baby me, they might have saved Salmon's life.

Sam shushes me gently, like a soothing lullaby. "We don't know for sure that he would've lived."

"I can't help but think that's what the deceiver was talking about when he mentioned me not learning my whole story, that I supposedly killed your dad?"

He cringes. "I remember the whole story, and it's not what you think."

"Tell me what you know."

———

Sam

How do I share without her taking the blame? If I'd tried to warn my dad when I saw him in the woods, he might've lived. Then again, how can I assume nothing else would've happened?

"Bahar went through *what if* in the past to save my dad's life and decided not to hide on Jimmy's farm. It worked. Salmon lived for a while after, but then when Bahar disappeared...."

"She still left even though Salmon was alive?" she asks.

"She found you," I say. "No matter how many times she relives the past, she finds you."

"Then why hasn't your dad been alive all these years?"

I breathe in, hold for a moment, then brace myself. "Because you changed the past."

Pero pauses mid-stroll, letting go of my hand. The space against my palm feels empty without her.

"How is that possible?" she asks. "Salmon would've been alive beforehand."

"If the past is changed too drastically or too often, it can erase a person's existence. Because I chose to walk away from my dad instead of trying to fix what might've happened, everything returned to our present reality. Our moms switched places raising us, Carper experimented on Bahar, and Salmon died."

Pero's eyes bulge. "You allowed your dad's death in order to redeem my past?"

"He may have died, anyway."

"But you let it happen, knowing if you hadn't, I may not have ever entered your life. You fought an internal battle. For me."

I could tell her it was nothing, but that wouldn't be true. Letting go of past pain isn't easy, even if it's to be with the one I love. "Elohim is the beginning and ending of our stories. I can't cling to a chapter that isn't mine to write."

"You have such peace, Sam. How can I trust Elohim will do the same for me?" She chokes on her words.

"Call on the great redeemer, and He'll come running, like I will. Because He loves you."

She tilts her head. "When I entered this *what if* world, I questioned who I was in it. But my identity isn't rooted in my past or future. I'm rooted in Elohim."

I nod. "Our Creator is constant, steadfast. All creation cries out to Him, and He never fails to help."

She holds onto the feather pendant, a normal dull brown. "Thank you for returning my heart. It's a joy to love you."

A thrill rushes through me, goosebumps surfacing on my arms. "Do you feel pressured to say that?"

She shakes her head. "I want to marry you, but I'm scared."

"Of what?"

"I recognized our passion for each other the moment I laid eyes on you. If something were to get in our way...."

I kiss her forehead, the corner of her lips, the tip of her nose. "Don't be afraid."

She closes her eyes and sighs.

Between kisses on her face, I whisper that I love her.

She shudders, fear diminishing with each touch.

The pounding of my heart prompts me to get down on one knee. Pulling out a ring from my pocket that's been waiting for a moment like this, I present it to her. I'm at her mercy, one answer away from a commitment. "No life is long enough to express my love for you, but I promise to honor and serve you as if each day is eternal. Pero Ruth Moshe, marry me?"

With a quick intake of breath, her hands hide her face as she nods. "Absolutely!" She extends a trembling hand, wiping tears from her face with the other.

I place the ring on her finger and stand while she holds it in front of her, tilting to view it from multiple angles. The ring is dark oak wood with a tiny diamond embedded in the middle.

"Sam, this is beautiful."

"I can make a new one if the band doesn't fit."

"You made this?" She places her hand against my chest, examining it more closely, with wide eyes and a smile. "Perfect."

"So are you."

She locks her gaze on me, her hand moving from my chest to around my waist. "Not at all."

"You're perfect to me."

She giggles. "I'll take it."

It's my turn to laugh when I think of the word she used when answering my proposal.

"What's so funny?"

"The word *absolutely* never sounded so sad."

She smacks my arm playfully. "Salmon Boaz Nesim! Those were happy tears, and I am nothing like jazzy Jace."

My laughter dies down as I bring my arms around her. Nuzzling my face against her neck, I whisper in her ear. "Thank you."

"For what?" Her voice is raspy.

"For being you."

When she brings her arms around my neck and draws me closer, I learn that to be held by a woman is to live in the goodness of Elohim.

29

PERO

For not being transporters, Sam and I have moved around a lot. In front of my old house in Green Meadow, Sam proposed and put a ring on my finger, but in a flash, we found ourselves in Origo, right in the middle of the Lesaries' camp.

The sky is bright blue, the air dry. Patches of brush and cacti scatter along the desert terrain. Ahead, a deep narrow valley trails in-between red-rock cliffs. Of all the places they could've settled, did it have to be the hottest? At least the soil is no longer charred, and a few plants are green, not shriveled and black. Life is back to both worlds.

I'm grateful to be out of *what if* and with our people, if we aren't in another past reality. Based on the gathering of children with dropped jaws and the houses being built all around us, I'm guessing we're in the present. Well, present for Origo. With all that traveling, who knows what year it is on Earth?

"Pro!" The small voice comes from a little girl, Lily, who never could pronounce my name. Her short legs scurry over, and she wraps her arms around me.

"Hi, Lily." I squat so that I'm face-to-face. "You've grown taller."

"You were gone for months!" She moves her arms out wide for expression. "Then you came from the sky!"

I chuckle. "It was days for me, but it feels longer." I'm about to ask a four-year-old what she thinks about my new ring but stop myself. Mom and Dad should see it first. "Have you seen my parents?"

She points a chubby finger toward a cabin.

"Thank you, Lily." I rub her head, then stand to join Sam while she skips away.

"You never told me you're good with kids."

"I wasn't around kids much until I joined the Lesaries. I've known Lily since she was a baby."

"You'll make a great mom someday."

A grin spreads wide. I hadn't considered being a mother much, but now that I'm about to be married, I'm looking forward to meeting little Sam's and Pero's. "And you'll make a great dad."

He leans close to my ear. "Can't we get married today?" His whining makes him fit right in with the surrounding crowd.

I shake my head, a smile escaping. "Not going to happen. I'd at least like a nice dress to wear for our wedding."

"That'll take months to make."

"I'll find one to borrow."

"So, tomorrow?"

I roll my eyes, then grab his hand and tug. "First, let's find our families."

"And Shea."

"Right away, eager boy. I swear, you sound so much like me. I had no idea you could get impatient."

"Hey. I have legit reasons."

After giving his hand a light squeeze, I lean against his shoulder. "I promise to be worth the wait."

His face turns a light pink. *Ha! Made him blush.*

We approach a cabin.

"You think this is the right place?" I ask.

"Let's find out."

I tap on the front door, then scan the solid wood structure. "It's neat to see the Lesaries finally settle down. Make sidewalks and it'll feel like a real neighborhood."

"They've done a good job building the houses." Sam studies the wood, brushing a hand against it.

"Maybe you can build one for us."

His eyes brighten. "I like the way you think."

I'm about ready to knock again when the door slides open. Bahar pauses before realizing who's in front of her. With a gasp, she pulls me into her embrace.

"Pero!" She lets go and scans me. "Your complexion is glowing. Really, you look amazing. And you beat that ugly storm. Cathena told me all about it."

So, Cathena had made it okay. That's a relief.

"It's so good to see you, Mom."

She turns to Sam and gives him a tight hug. "What've you two been up to?" Releasing, she studies Sam, then laughs. "You've never been more handsome, Salmon. Like your dad. Pero laid at your feet, didn't she?"

"Mom!" I shake my head while holding out my hand to show the evidence.

Sam laughs along with her. "Pero did lay at my feet, but I also proposed."

"Way to be persistent! Ooh." She brings the ring close to her face. "Hard to see well without my glasses." She steps from out of the home and closes the door behind her, never letting go of my hand. "It's clearly Nesim carpentry work. Good work, Sam."

"Thanks, Mom."

It still sounds strange for him to call Bahar *mom*, but I suppose when two mothers accidentally swap their kids, we both have reason to call each other's mom's by that title. You'd think this would make our family dynamic more complicated. In my head, it's more simplified. Kind of like when a set of sisters marries a set of brothers. Why must a family tree split in multiple directions when you can share a single stump?

"Since when do you wear glasses?" I ask Mom.

She grins. "You'd think you were gone longer than six months. I've been squinting lately. Good thing the supplies from Earth included reading glasses. Don't ask how they got the right prescription."

My smile fades, one question burning in my heart. "Where's Dad? Has he fully recovered?"

"Your dad's fine."

Then why is she frowning?

"He had a stroke," she says.

I puff out the rising tension with a breath of air. "Recently?"

"Apparently he'd already had it without realizing. It caused high fever, pneumonia, and other long-term effects."

"Like what?" Beads of sweat trail down my spine, and it can't be from the midday heat alone.

"He's lost some memory. Everyday things, not his family. He also has paralysis on one side of his body."

"Oh, no!" Pins and needles travel through my hands.

"Permanently?" Sam asks.

"It comes and goes, so it's hard to say at this point."

"Poor Dad." At fifty-five, he's too young for a stroke. Thank Elohim he's alive, but I feel for him having to experience this kind of pain.

"I'm sorry to hear this happened." Sam appears genuinely concerned. "Is there a way we can help Matthew's recovery?"

Right there is another reason I love this man. Matthew isn't Sam's father, while Bahar is his biological mother. Bitterness could be a result after his dad died, his mom disappeared from his life, remarried, and adopted me as her own daughter.

Instead, he's offering to help and marry into the very family who left him.

"Prayers are the most helpful."

"I never had a chance to find medicine," I say. "From your letter, I assumed he was fine."

Mom shakes her head. "I'm not sure medicine would help him at this point. Besides, you had more important matters to attend to." She waggles her brows. "But your dad would love to walk you down the aisle."

A melancholy feeling settles in my heart. Of course he'll walk me down the aisle, even if it takes a crutch, wheelchair, or my shoulder to lean on. "I can't imagine anyone else." My stomach thuds when my other dad comes to mind. My *Bàba*. "I'd like to ask Dad if he'd mind me including one more."

"It's kind of you to consider Carper." Mom's smile is sad, as if she's unsure he deserves an invitation to such a momentous occasion. But my relationship with Carper differs from hers. I didn't suffer from the trauma of his abuse like she did, so I'll never fully understand her perspective, especially when he's proven himself reliable and caring.

The sound of a door opening has us turn to find Dad leaning in the entryway. "Bahar, have you seen—?" He stalls, searching my face as if to check in his mind for recognition. When his features brighten, I run up to him and share a hug, careful not to hurt him.

He's frail, with pasty skin despite the bright sun. The right side of his body droops slightly, and his eyes have lost their shimmer, yet with me beside him, I catch a flash of spark followed by a pool of tears.

"Pero, is it really you?"

"Hi, Dad." I reach on tip-toes and kiss his cheek. What previously was clean shaven is replaced with a full-length, bushy beard with specks of gray. "A beard looks good on you."

Crinkled eyes and facial hair moving upward indicate a smile. "See, Bahar?"

Mom chuckles. "Don't encourage him, Pero."

Dad's laugh is hearty, telling me abundant life still courses through his blood.

Sam folds his arms. "What do you think, babe?" He strokes his stubbled jawline.

Butterflies flutter inside for two reasons. First, he called me *babe*. Besides calling me *Ruth*, this is the first term of endearment he's used for me. Second, I really liked it. "Then what would I use as a scratch post?"

Mom throws her arms out dramatically. "That's what I always tell Matthew."

Dad chuckles. "TMI, ladies."

A broad smile lingering on my lips, I turn toward Dad while he remains leaning against the house for support.

"You and that guy, huh?"

I nod, a wave of panic pulsating through my veins. "Do you remember him?"

"How could I forget? Sam leaves a good impression on everyone he meets."

I sigh in relief. As Sam approaches and places an arm around me, I lean against him.

"Thanks again for your blessing, Matthew."

I swerve toward Sam. "You talked with my dad beforehand?"

"I asked permission before he was sick."

"Such faith," I say.

"I was determined."

"It paid off."

"Hate to interrupt a thing between you two," Dad says, "but I'm not used to standing and could use a seat. Come inside, and we can talk more."

I take in the space of about 800 square feet. To my right, the living room and kitchen are adjacent. One bedroom is straight ahead, and around the corner is another room and bathroom, the tiny hall holding a stacked washer and dryer. A window-unit air conditioner sits in the living room, whirling with a gentle hum.

I give a low whistle. "Origo is moving up."

Dad settles into a wooden rocking chair, the same one from the cabin where Sam once lived. More than likely, Salmon made it for Mom years ago. Did they bring furniture from that cabin all the way here? Talk about determination.

"Yeah," Dad says, "everything involving electricity is Carper's doing."

"Carper was here?" I settle on the wool rug, grazing my hand against its scratchy texture. Sam sits beside me.

"Take this chair, Pero." Mom points to the other piece of furniture, not as exquisite in craftsmanship as Salmon's work, but functional. "I'm going to find Shea and Alexis, tell them you're here."

Interesting that she hurries to leave immediately after Carper's name is mentioned again. Did something recently happen between them or is her mind fixed on the past?

"Sounds great," Sam says. "I want to speak to Shea right away."

I withhold a snort. He can't bear a night without asking Shea to marry us. It's a wonderful feeling to be desired so much. Makes me long for him in return. I shake my head to clear the thoughts. Maybe we *should* get married tomorrow.

"Are you all right, Ruth?" Sam's watching me and the blush that no doubt has my face beet red.

"Yes. Umm, yeah. Everything's completely normal up here." I point to my head. "What was the question?"

He smirks. "There was no question. Just a faraway look in your eye."

"It was nothing. Well, it wasn't exactly nothing, like I don't care or something because I totally do." I rub my cheeks, hoping the heat lingering there will settle down. "Anyway, Dad, you mentioned Carper was here. When was that?"

Dad clears his throat as if taking my cue to move on. "About a month ago. He came with supplies to install the air-conditioners, outlets, and other appliances. Trained several Lesaries to complete this task themselves using solar panels. We have an entire community settling here. Looks like the traveling's done and we're rooting ourselves as the tribe of Judah."

"I think I've met Judah," I say.

Sam nods. "You have. Judah often shares about his past. At one point, he sold his younger brother into slavery because he didn't like him. Later on, he fathered twin boys from a woman quite a few years younger than him, who happened to be his daughter-in-law."

"Wow. I thought my life was complicated."

"This was before Elohim turned Judah's life completely around," Sam says.

I shake my head in disbelief. "Doesn't sound much different from Carper's story."

"It's not, really," Dad says. "When Elohim redeems His people, they have all kinds of histories. Speaking of stories, I have something to share that you may not be aware of."

Not another secret! Will the drama ever end?

"Would you like to sit, Pero?" Dad extends a hand toward the nearby chair.

"No, I'm fine on the floor. The rug is comfortable." I'm reminded of a similar one back home in Green Meadow, how I used to sit cross-legged on the smooth texture and trace the swirled design. Our old house was small, but this house is even smaller. Somehow, it suits Dad. He appears settled in Salmon's rocking chair. It doesn't feel like he's replaced him, more like Salmon has given Matthew his blessing to be the king of this house. Dad has stepped into his role with confidence and grace.

Dad shifts. "Your mom and I have different memories involving the same person. She's under the impression you won't remember this change, so I thought it would be good to prepare you."

I glance at Sam, bracing myself for the heavy news.

"Henry and Cathena are married."

I slap my hands on the floor. "What?"

"When?" Sam's tone is lower, as if he's jealous Henry beat him to it.

"Nearly a year ago."

I shake my head. "Not possible. Cathena and I traveled with the Lesaries a year ago while Henry was studying medicine in China."

"Hmm," Dad says. "Sounds like your mom was right."

"About what?"

"The past."

Sam raises a brow. Seems like this relates to the *what if* world.

"Bahar says my memory isn't always accurate after the stroke," Dad says, "but I distinctly remember when we were in our old home in Green Meadow, right before we were taking off to find Bahar and Henry. While you two went for a walk, Carper checked on you. He called me over to the window, and we both witnessed Sam on one knee and the obvious yes from Pero."

My face had finally cooled off when it heats up again. "You spied on us?"

"Guilty." Dad takes a drink of water from a nearby cup. "Carper and I ended up heading to China by ourselves to find your mom. When we got there, we eventually found Bahar but not Henry. We later learned he'd ended up landing in our same old house in Green Meadow and left to find Cathena. After they were married, I gave them the house to live in since I don't use it anymore."

"That's not what I was expecting." I puff out a breath I'd been holding. "What's Mom's story?"

"Sam stayed behind, and you and Henry fell in love. You broke up shortly after, but not before Henry stole your heart."

I gasp. Had I been the last to find out about what Henry did?

"How'd you hear about that?" Sam asks.

Dad looks at Sam, then at me. "When you left from Origo, your mom found your necklace on the ground. She said the bright blue feather showed someone had stolen your heart. You needed to be redeemed by Sam if you really loved him. She was confident you did."

I bite my lower lip. If I never traveled to the Forbidden City, I was never in a dungeon with Carper. Without extra months spent with him, would we be as close as we are now? Would I have discovered he's my biological father?

"Why mention this right when we get here?" Couldn't Dad have waited till we'd caught up a little? I feel like I'm going from bliss to a nightmare in a matter of minutes.

"I had to before you run into Henry."

"Why would I do that?"

Dad sighs. "Because he's here."

I sit up straighter. "*Here*, here?"

"With the Lesaries, not inside the house. He and Cathena transported to Origo this morning."

"What for?"

Dad shrugs. "From what I understand, they aren't sure yet. Elohim transported them here."

Right before my wedding, I'll have to face Henry. Why else would they be here if not for me to straighten things out? Sam addressed the conflict with Henry, but I never finished the conversation. I'm not bitter that two of my greatest friends married each other. But I don't want any past distractions in the way of my happiness with Sam. I guess I thought it'd be a happily ever after from yesterday forward, till death do us part. Now things are different because Sam proposed. It wasn't his fault. How could he foresee a proposal altering the wrinkles of time?

"One more thing to mention," Dad says. "Right after Carper and I saw your proposal, you both disappeared out of thin air."

Resting my face in my hands, I groan, then lift my head to Sam, who looks equally exasperated. "We changed history."

30

———————

SAVE

PERO

A flurry of excited voices mingles in Mom and Dad's living room. After exchanging hugs with Shea and Alexis, we all catch up. The group oohs and aahs over my ring and asks plenty of questions. Did I receive Shea's letter? How did we find each other? Was it love at third sight?

But I can't get our talk with Dad out of my head. Concern niggles my thoughts, pestering me with *what if*s, and I'm not even in that dreaded place anymore. Sam was right to caution me about staying there. If only we'd left sooner. There I go again, trapped by past choices when I really should focus on the present.

A couple of hours later, Shea and Alexis leave, Sam with them to talk with Shea alone. Dad goes to his room for a nap, and Mom makes dinner. Asking Mom if I can borrow a phone (they have both the latest and most ancient technology), I excuse myself to the guest room. First priority, a long-distance call.

He answers right away. "Calvin speaking."

I smile. "Not Dr. Carper anymore?"

A pause. "Who is this?"

"Pero. Who else?"

Another pause. "Pero Moshe?"

"The very one. Although...." I extend my hand to catch a glimpse of the precious jewel sparkling in the light. "Soon to be Pero Nesim. Or Ruth Nesim. Whichever you prefer."

"As in Salmon Nesim?" Carper asks. "Didn't he die? Oh, wait. He had a son, right?"

"Why this sudden interest in asking questions?"

"Do you have a problem with that?"

"Yes," I say.

Silence. "Did you call me just to ask why I'm asking questions?"

"Another inquiry."

"I'm hanging up now," he says.

"Bàba, wait!"

More silence.

"Are you still there?" I ask.

"Yeah." A sigh. "Trying to figure out why you called me *dad* in Mandarin."

My turn to sigh. Carper doesn't know. We're not friends, despite his care for me in Moon City and the Forbidden City.

I ignore his curiosity and plunge into what I long to know. "What happened between us?"

"People part ways, Pero. It's part of life. I went to China, and you took off with the first guy to pop the question. Not the kind *I* ask, but *the* question." The timbre in his voice changes. "Oh, I get it. You're about to be a Nesim because you're marrying that young man named Sam. It's coming back to me, but that was years ago."

"I'll explain every—"

"You haven't told me why you called me *Bàba*," he says. "Seems a little personal, don't you think?"

Here we go again. Another long tale to share, plus the

uncertainty that he'll believe it. "I'll tell you everything, but before I do, I have a question."

"I thought you didn't like questions."

"That was a lie, because this is the biggest request I've ever asked of you."

He clears his throat. "Go for it."

"Would you do me the honor of walking me down the aisle?"

No response.

"With Matthew, too, of course," I add.

Nothing.

"Hello? Did you hang up on me?"

"I'm here." His voice breaks. "Just processing."

"Would it help if I gave more context?"

"Perhaps."

"Okay." I sigh. "How do I say this? You are...you're my father by blood."

A shuffling noise sounds from the background. "How?"

"Does DNA alteration through surrogation ring a bell?"

He growls low. "Yeah."

"Involving a woman named Alexis?"

"I remember."

He sounds sad, regretful maybe. His reaction differs drastically from his initial response.

I dive into our history, sharing every nook and cranny of the narrative I long to return to. Sam could've proposed after we left *what if*. Then Carper would've remembered us singing to Elohim while in jail, him rescuing me from being buried, the banters, encouragement, and laughter. The treasured memories that make a family and keep it. Without my *bàba*, I'd lose a bit of my roots all over again. As if Mom left me anew. Like another stolen heart.

"I'll think about it." His voice still rings a sad tone. "This is a lot to take in, and I'm in the middle of a breakthrough with an experiment."

"Not on people, I hope."

"Never again on anyone but myself."

"You're experimenting on yourself?" I ask.

"Every day. The theory is called Longevity Escape Velocity. It's all the rage with top scientists today. If all goes according to plan, I'll live until I'm two-hundred, perhaps forever."

"I'm not going to lie," I say. "Being immortal doesn't sound too exciting. A face that old would make babies cry."

"Thanks."

"You're welcome."

"Look, Pero. I better get going."

Hint for being over this conversation. But I'm not done. "Where did you end up settling?"

"Your hometown," he says.

"In Green Meadow, huh?"

"Exactly what I said."

"Weren't you planning on becoming king of the Lesaries in Green Meadow?" I ask.

"It's kind of hard to be king over a deserted sanctuary."

"You were there during the storms when everyone evacuated?"

He doesn't answer. "It was great hearing from you, Pero. Congratulations on your engagement."

"Thanks," I say. "We'll have to talk more later." There are more details I'm dying to find out. How much of the past did Sam and I change?

"Sure," he responds.

Not gonna happen.

"I'll let you go, Carper."

I think I hear a sigh, as if he's relieved I'm not calling him Dad. As if his invention could make a daughter vanish the second he hangs up. I'll return to *Pero*. Not his Pero. Just *Pero*, a girl he used to care for.

"Before you leave," I say, "I'd like to caution you about this experiment of yours. Remember the man you used to be? Power can easily turn to greed, and nothing good comes from thinking life owes you."

"I appreciate the warning."

"The deceiver is real and causes all sorts of doubts. I met him myself. His name is Rife, like the furniture store."

"I'm not worried," Carper says.

"Another thing. You should consider becoming a musician. You wouldn't get paid much, but hey, the sound is good."

"I learned piano when I was young," he says, "but that kind of life isn't for me, thank you."

"Understood." I pause. "Carper?"

"What?" He's impatient, annoyed.

"Please, at least consider coming to my wedding. It would mean so much to me."

"I'll consider it. I'm hanging up now. Okay?"

"Kay."

"Goodbye, Pero."

"Bye."

I press the red circle to end the call, feeling less like a woman soon to become a bride and more like a little girl waiting for her daddy to come home.

What if he never does?

31

SPEAK

SAM

Shea's ready to marry us whenever we're ready. Which would've been a week ago if it were up to me. We felt it wise to wait. But a month? It can't come fast enough!

Lately, I've considered following the Lesarien custom for marriage. I talked with Pero about it, but she wasn't so sure. I'd be away for up to a year, securing a place to live. When I'd return for Pero, a whole parade of men would carry me on their shoulders, shouting out my arrival. The tradition is beautiful and enhances the anticipation to make her mine. A promise to return, a blissful reunion, entering a new home made by my own hands.

What follows the parade would be awkward for Pero. The bride and groom enter a house and consummate the marriage before leaving for their own home. The Lesaries linger outside of the house, then celebrate when the couple walks out together. I'm not bothered by this part of the custom, but it might seem strange to those who don't want everyone knowing about the intimate details of their lives.

If we did follow the Lesarien custom, I could hire workers to make building a house faster. But do I have the stamina to wait for six months before having sex with my wife? American's modern-day wedding traditions sound much more appealing. Following the ceremony, a lavish, secluded resort awaits. A romantic getaway for two. *Heavenly.*

Shea's excited to see his investment in me and Pero come to completion. Of course, he's aware life won't be perfect once we're married. Post-honeymoon, reality will sink in. Trust and communication will be the driving factors of our commitment to each other.

"Receive the counsel," he says.

So, here we are in Shea and Alexis's home, gathering their words of wisdom and settling them in our hearts. They both were married much later in years, yet their experiences, both single and married, give them an advantage for counseling.

I'm ready to learn and apply. Oh, so ready!

Pero

I want to appreciate and understand all that I can about Sam, but since we arrived in Origo a week ago, I've been on a roller-coaster of emotions. Excitement for getting married, trepidation on if I'll ever see Carper again, and anxiety over the fact that I've run into Henry nearly every day, but haven't addressed our past relationship.

Henry and Cathena are well-matched. Finally, a woman has come whose looks intimidate him as much as Henry's intimidates everyone else. Yet it's more than Cathena's beauty that has his head spinning. Her fiery personality calms his hyperactivity in a positive way. He's more grounded yet still fun-loving and adventurous.

Cathena and I are rebuilding our friendship, but with a different past, it's like starting all over.

Sam squeezes my hand, awakening me from a daydream.

"Is it all right with you if I bring up your concerns?" He calmly asks, willing to drop it if I don't care to talk with Shea and Alexis, yet concerned for my well-being.

I nod my head. "Yeah, go ahead."

Fingers interlaced with mine, Sam gives my hand another squeeze before turning toward our company. "Pero's been struggling with a lot of anxiety lately." He turns to me. "Do you want to tell them? I won't speak for you unless you'd like me to."

Will Sam always be so caring? His kindness toward me is almost unbearable, in a good way. "I can share."

Alexis and Shea wait patiently.

"I'm concerned about my relationships right now. I guess I'll start with Carper."

Shea nods.

"I'm afraid I've lost him forever," I say. "Realizing he could be absent from my life revealed how much he means to me as a father. I shouldn't love him. He harmed my family, after all. Yet we've been through so much together. He changed, but when I talked with him on the phone, he wasn't the same. He was cold and callous, practically begging to get off the phone with me. What if he's become the person he used to be?"

"We can't control others," Shea says. "Who we become depends on our own choices."

I let go of Sam's hand to shift in the chair. "I wonder if our shared experiences helped Carper become a better person."

Shea fixates on the ceiling. "It's possible Elohim used you to make a positive influence on Carper, which could've caused his faith to grow. Although, Carper eventually had to face a choice if he would continue to follow Elohim's wisdom, or forge his own path."

I place a hand on my chest. "I've made stupid decisions, even recently, but it hasn't made me bitter."

"There's the difference," Shea says. "You recognize the

wrong direction for your life, and you desire to make better choices in the future. You've turned away from mistakes and live by Elohim's forgiveness and grace."

Carper's lack of humility is similar to being in a *what if* state indefinitely. The difference is as clear as colors versus gray. I choose to turn away from my past mistakes, not conjuring up the possibilities of what could've been. Whether Carper prefers the same is up to him.

Alexis lifts a hand tentatively. "Can I mention something? An observation, really."

"Of course," I say.

"When Dr. Carper came to help us out with the houses, he acted differently. A lot of complaining and short temper. I wondered if he was upset about his daughter Cherry and her family moving on with another tribe. But from what I observed, Dr. Carper's temper is getting the best of him again. Something is going on in his personal life to drive him toward this behavior. Pero, I don't think this has anything to do with your actions. Who he becomes is not your fault."

"Are you sure it wasn't Carper's personality coming through?" I ask. "Not everyone gets his sarcasm."

"It was harsher than joking around." Alexis grimaces, as if hesitating to say more. "I understand your relationship with him is important to you, but maybe it's best to lean on caution in this case and not push for him to attend the wedding."

Aha. I understand why Mom acted so strangely when Carper's name was mentioned. An ache throbs in my chest. I can't imagine letting go of my other dad if he's still within reach. "Is it alright to call him occasionally?"

"I don't see the harm." Alexis looks toward her husband. "Shea?"

"If he's still open to it, there's no harm in having conversations with your biological father. But I encourage you to check how those calls impact you afterward, especially as you're heading into the start of your own family. Your relationship with Sam and Elohim are the two most important. If staying in contact with Carper negatively affects that bond, then you might consider distancing yourself. Every so often, forgiveness involves setting boundaries."

"That makes sense." My heart feels heavier, yet the answer brings peace.

"We're here for you, Pero," Shea says.

"Thank you." I grab Sam's hand again, tears surfacing. "I'm overwhelmed by how much you all love me. You're like family to me."

"That's the beauty of Elohim's people," Alexis says. "When we're united in Elohim, there is power."

Hadn't I learned that repeatedly? Being a Lesarie wasn't about selfish gain or satisfying my every need; we're one body. With that comes correction, insight, grace, and love.

Sam

Pero and I exit the door from our counseling session when Cathena calls out our names.

"Hey!" Cathena runs up, Henry right behind. "You two wanna help us watch some kids tonight?"

Henry joins our mini circle. "I'm sure they're busy getting ready for their wedding, Cat."

I glance at Pero. "We might be up to it." I could use more opportunities around children since I'd like to have my own someday. Maybe in a few years. "What are you watching kids for?"

"Some parents are going out tonight and need more helpers to watch their kids. It'll be a wild evening with ten of them."

"Ten kids!" When Pero and I talked about how many children we'd like, we both agreed on two or three. While not all ten belong to the same set of parents, picturing watching that many kids in one house makes me nervous.

"We're in." Pero sounds confident. The crossing of her arms and the slit of her eyes show she has an idea.

"Excellent." Cathena gives us high-fives. "Six o'clock at the Norris's house. They're the ones who live—"

I nod my head. "I've been to their house before."

"Yay!" She holds onto Pero's hands. "This will be so much fun. We could get to know each other more."

"That will be great." Pero's smile appears fake.

"We need to get the food ready." Cathena turns. "See you tonight."

Henry beats a fist on his chest twice, then holds out two fingers in a *v*. "Catch you later, bruh."

"Peace out." I nod once. Funny how I adopt Gen-Z idioms whenever I'm around Henry, but as soon as he leaves, I speak like I'm historic. "Wait!"

Henry swivels on his heel. "What's up?"

"Out of curiosity, where do couples go for a date in the wilderness?"

"That's what eagles are for."

I laugh. "Where could an eagle fly someone around here that's so exciting?"

He tilts his head. "Woods, oceans, mountain tops, clouds. Nature's a bussin' playground."

I fold my arms, my grin wide. "It sure is."

Henry leaves.

No one knows nature's tendencies as much as I do, having dealt with fierce weather for months. As dangerous as exploring nature can be, it's also a wonder. Maybe I'll build a house for Pero on her landscape of choice. I can imagine the look on her face if I surprised her with a home near the edge of a hilltop overlooking a valley.

"What are you thinking about?" she asks.

I sigh, wrapping her in my arms. "Our future."

She sinks into my embrace. I cherish when she collapses into this posture, as if there's no place she'd rather be. "Is it looking bright?"

"Very." I kiss her forehead. "Now, what were *you* thinking when you signed us up to babysit?"

"That we should have ten kids of our own."

My arms tense. "Don't tell me you're serious."

She giggles. "I'm not."

"Good, because I was about to ask you if we should consider one instead."

"Do you realize how lonely being an only child can be?"

"Does it have to be?" I ask. "We currently live in a tight community."

"True." She releases from my hold. "You'd rather stay *here*, instead of Earth?"

"I think so. What about you?"

She tilts her head. "Yeah. Being around Lesaries feels homey. It's hotter here than I prefer, but I'll get used to it. I never did like Oregon's rain."

"It's settled, then. I'll search for some land, but not near our parents, please. As much as I love them, I'd rather not wake up to a knock on my door every morning."

She shakes her head, a smile on her lips. "They wouldn't do that."

I raise a brow. "You haven't been around Alexis much."

"After everything she said in counseling about boundaries?"

"Yes, but when Alexis makes her famous bread, there's no stopping her from barging into homes to share a loaf."

She laughs out loud. "Now, *that* I believe."

I take her hand and lead her toward Bahar and Matthew's home. We've been eating there for lunch and at Alexis and Shea's place for dinner, except for the couple of occasions when

Lesarien families invited us to share a meal with them. Each night, I stay with a bunch of single guys who share a house, and Pero stays with her parents. They've all reassured us they don't mind us joining them, but it will be nice when we don't have to share a kitchen or steal a room. We go for walks as often as possible to be alone.

"Why did you really sign us up for tonight?" I'm certain the reason involves Henry.

Pero twirls her hair. Since when did she restart that nervous habit? "I plan on talking with him."

I agree, suppressing the thought that this task shouldn't be so hard. Pero's different from me. She must come to her own decisions. "I'm proud of you for being so brave."

"But?"

Does she hear my hesitation?

"Are you sure starting a serious discussion is a good idea with ten kids running around?"

She shrugs. "Didn't think about that. Maybe after?"

"Probably depends on how tired we are."

She sighs. "Then how about now?"

"They're busy preparing." Still, it would be nice to get it out of the way.

"We can help them, then tell them we'd like to talk."

"Alright. Let's try."

Pero

After eating lunch, we walk over to Henry and Cathena's place. The Lesaries built a few empty houses, so Henry and Cathena temporarily live in this one until they return to Earth. For transporters, no one's ever certain when that will be.

Sam knocks on the door. A thousand knots form in my

stomach. *Why am I making such a big deal out of this? It's not like talking with Henry will change my mind about Sam.*

Henry opens the door. "Hey, guys! What's happening?"

When I can't get myself to say anything, Sam jumps in. "We were hoping to talk with you. Everything's okay, but something's on our minds we'd like to share."

"Okay, yeah. No prob." He opens the door wide.

I clear my throat. "We can wait if now's not convenient." I take a couple of steps backward.

"Nah." Henry nods his head, inviting us in. "Everything's ready for tonight, and we're free for a few hours."

As we walk through, a black kitten meows, sauntering toward the open door. Henry grabs it at the last moment.

"Stone." He holds it close. "You don't belong out there."

Cathena's called Cat, while their cat's name is Stone. How adorable!

"Cute kitty." I pet it, a small, soft cushion.

"Thanks. We've had her for a few weeks." He brings Stone closer to me. "Luckily, she came with us when we transported to Origo. Would you like a turn?"

"Sure." I lift her from his hands. Stone's barely longer than my palm. Her tiny paws swat around, feet wiggling in the air. "She's so sweet."

"You can set her down, if you'd like."

"I'll hold her a little longer." *If she's near while I talk, I'll get through this much easier.* "Sam, feel her fur."

He gives her a pet.

"Isn't she soft?"

"Yep."

He doesn't seem too enthused. *I'm okay with that. More kitty cuteness to myself.*

"Have a seat." Henry motions to the couch, then pulls up a chair from their kitchen table. "Cathena!"

"Yeah," she calls from another room.

"I'll get her." Henry leaves while we sit.

A minute later, they both enter.

"Hello, again," Cathena says. "Henry says you want to talk."

So, we're plunging right into it. I gently stroke the kitten, who has fallen asleep on my lap.

"Yes." I clear my throat. "I want to discuss mine and Henry's past relationship."

Cathena and Henry's heads swivel toward each other as they lock widened eyes.

Cathena looks at me. "What relationship?"

Henry scratches his head. "I was wondering the same thing."

I was so concerned about having hurt Henry's feelings, I didn't consider he wouldn't remember dating.

Sam and I explain the situation, how we'd changed history and Henry had stolen my heart. That Sam had to win it back. How I'd never found closure when he gave my heart back.

When we're finished, Henry lets out a big breath. "Wow. I'm not sure what to say. Pero, when I was your bodyguard in high school, I admit I had a crush on you. But when I saw the way you and Sam looked at each other, I backed off. It hurt a little, but you're familiar with how crushes go. In the end, they're nothing more. Seldom do they turn into something more. Except for this marvelous lady." He gives Cathena a wink.

Cathena blows him a kiss, then turns back to us as if recalling she has an audience. "I noticed a similar thing on the roof when you two first met. I've never seen anyone fall in love so quickly before. It was obvious you would be together someday. Can't say it was the same for Henry and me." She smiles. "Took me a while to grow up."

"Ha!" Henry grins. "I was way less mature than you, Cat."

Totally accurate, or at least involving the Henry I used to know. His maturity shone through in his decision to give me up for Sam. Finally, a change from the past worked in our favor.

Would I have fallen in love with Sam first if Henry hadn't kissed me? I'd like to think I would've since Henry backed away.

Henry studies me. "I'm sorry your memory involves me stealing your heart. I shouldn't have taken away your freedom to choose. You weren't mine to keep."

My muscles relax in relief. His response is key to unlocking my tension. "I forgive you."

With those three words, the burden vanishes.

So do Henry and Cathena, disappearing in a flash, their cat still sound asleep on my lap.

Sam snickers. "I'll never get used to that."

"I guess they really were here because we needed to talk."

"How are you feeling?" Sam asks.

"Great! No, guilty I kept their kitten." Selfishly, I want to keep Stone. How would we send her back, anyway? Maybe Faith could carry her. A cat riding on an eagle. What a funny picture.

Sam smirks. "I'm also wondering who will occupy this house if Henry and Cathena are no longer around to live in it."

I gasp. "Brilliant!"

He hesitates. "Unless we follow the Lesarien tradition. I kind of have my heart set on building my own."

"We could ask Judah if it's available, in case Plan A doesn't work out."

He nearly jumps in excitement. "You're willing to wait for me to build?"

I shrug. "I'm not crazy about you being away for so many months, but I understand it means a lot to you. Something about you returning for me sounds incredibly romantic."

"Perfect." He gives a wide smile.

Happiness tugs at my heart-strings. For some unknown reason, following the Lesarien tradition feels like the right thing to do.

"I have one request." My eyes plead with him as I lean closer.

"Whatever's in my power to give you, I will." His eager face makes my insides twist. If I'm his queen, then he's my king. I don't hold power over him. We make decisions together.

"I'd like an American ceremony," I say. "I've dreamed of it since childhood. We'd have it along with the Lesarie's wedding tradition, of course."

"Done."

I pull away. "Will you always go along with my suggestions?" Come to think of it, he gave into my pleading in *what if*, even though he was reluctant to go through another door.

"It'd be good for you to make your own decisions, don't you think?"

Tilting my head, I fold my arms. "What if it's not a wise choice?"

"Then you'll learn from the consequences."

He's serious. "You'll allow me to suffer from foolish mistakes when you have the power to caution me?"

He cocks his brow. "Wouldn't it seem controlling if I tried to stop you?"

"Wouldn't it be controlling if I live my own life without first consulting with you?" I feel my face heat, my pulse rising. "We're a team, Sam. We'll need to work together."

"I get that." He sighs. "I guess I'm used to independence, making my own choices."

"That makes sense." I take a deep breath. "I'm used to verbally processing big things before I come to a conclusion. Unless it's a spur-of-the-moment thing, which is how all my dumb actions start."

He places an arm around my shoulder.

"How do we reconcile differences with such opposite personalities?" I ask.

"We'd be less okay if we agreed about everything. The question is, how do we move forward?"

I lean my head against his. "Accept our differences?"

"Yes. Maybe also make a plan on how to meet each other's needs."

"I give you some independence, and you talk through my decisions."

He nods. "And vice versa."

A knot in my stomach releases. "That makes me feel better."

"Good." He kisses my forehead. "I love you."

I'll never be tired of hearing those words. "I love you more."

He groans. "I just realized we're babysitting ten kids by ourselves tonight."

I burst with laughter. "Thanks to Henry and Cathena leaving."

"Yet, you're not scared." His tone playfully mocks.

"What's there to be afraid of? It will be an adventure."

"I guess when you put it that way."

Me. Sam. A full life ahead of us.

Onwerto.

32

VEIL

PERO

The sun's light shimmers through the window, washing over me. An eagerness to be Sam's bride tugs at my heart. A hand resting on the windowpane, I breathe in. Joy is in the air, Sam's warm breath on my face moments away. How did I arrive here? Weeks of preparation, years of sensing we belonged together. They all culminate at this point.

I've asked to be left alone for a minute before the ceremony starts. I'm learning to love the quiet places and myself in them.

I run a hand along the smooth fabric of my wedding gown, thankful to be in formal wear that isn't poofy or made of mulberry silk. The simple and enchanting lace overlay starts with a sweetheart neckline along the collarbone and cascades to the floor, a short train trailing behind. A waterfall of curls spills from a high bun, resting on my shoulders. I wear the necklace to remind me of *koach*. Some may wish for prosperity or eternal bliss before getting married, but I seek strength. In trials, which are bound to happen, I will turn to Elohim for strength in my marriage. He alone can make me truly happy.

Outside of the window, I notice a figure in the distance. I

squint, spotting Carper leaning heavily on one leg, arms folded. He's in a suit, tie and all.

"He made it!"

Carper turns around and walks toward two large rocks heading into the canyon. Is he unsure where the wedding is?

Gathering up my dress, I rush out the door. He's almost fully out of sight, about to step through a doorway filled with light. A cold sensation stops me in my tracks. He's not coming for me. He's leaving.

"Carper!" I yell out.

Mom and Alexis huddle nearby, silencing their chatting.

"What's going on, Pero?" Alexis asks.

I ignore her, grateful I decided on wearing white Nikes under the gown. Once a runner, always a runner.

"You're not taking off, are you?" Mom asks. "You'll completely ruin your dress."

That's exactly what I'm thinking. Clutching the train tighter in my grasp, I lean forward, my eyes set on Carper.

Run!

I've returned to my regular exercise schedule, so I catch up with him quickly and without being too out of breath. He hesitates at the open portal waiting for him to jump through. I can't believe he appeared, simply to leave me.

"Carper, wait!" I pause.

He doesn't turn; his shoulders tense.

"Why are you here?" I ask.

He sighs deeply, as if tenderness has risen from a fragile heart, and he's unsure how to push it down. "I don't know."

"You've come all this way. You might as well look at me."

He nods, then turns at last. When his gaze meets mine, his compressed shoulders ease.

I stagger back a step when I notice his face glistening with fresh tears. Why is he crying?

"You shouldn't be dragging that nice dress in the dirt." He

swats at his wet cheeks as if they are pesky flies. "You look stunning."

I smile. "You said the same thing to me when I had to wear your ridiculous choice of attire in Moon City. I nearly threw up."

He doesn't respond, not even a hint of a smile.

"That big, black dress?" I raise a brow.

"I remember."

"But you don't recall me being your daughter and the months we shared in China."

He shakes his head. "I wish I could be that man for you, whoever he was. Sounds like the father-type, the kind you deserve. Matthew is good for you. I'm not. I have to be the man I've always been."

"You *do* have a choice."

His face twitches. "I don't see possibilities like you do."

"Why not? Elohim can transform you into a better person. You'll become stronger. Gentle. Compassionate. Don't you want those things?"

"I do."

I grin. "Hey, I'm the one who's supposed to say those words today."

When he doesn't laugh or return with a better line, I sense he's done. It takes everything in me not to extend my hand, just to determine if he would latch onto it or withdraw. But my heart already has the answer.

"I can't," he says.

My fists tighten. "At least come celebrate the biggest day of my life. Please?"

He heads toward the doorway in the canyon. "Bye, Pero. Don't call me."

Now I'm the one crying. "You had to do this to me at my wedding? Of all days? Unbelievable."

With head cast down and a frown, he whispers. "I wish the

best for your marriage."

"Don't do this to me." My voice cracks.

He leaves.

I can only stand here. My hands droop at my sides, reminding me this world consists of shifting sand.

Peace. I have overcome the world.

And yet His gentle voice governs universes, galaxies, and the wildest of storms. He invites my soul to rest, to drink a sip of the life He offers and taste mercy.

What a good Father you are!

"Breathe in." Shea's deep tone comes from behind me, but it's as if he surrounds me, a tender voice pouring strength into my ears and ringing through my mind.

I obey.

"What do you smell?" he asks.

I let out a breath. "Something smokey, earthy. Also, a hint of Carper's cologne."

"Describe Carper's smell."

I grit my teeth. "Betrayal."

Shea steps forward to stand beside me. "Try again."

After an angry exhale, I take in another breath. "Mint and citrus tones. He smells rich. Important."

"Good. Now, what do you feel?"

"Hurt."

"I asked *what* you feel, not *how*."

If I were younger, I'd allow myself into a tantrum, but I've changed. Is sadness and rejection worth holding onto?

No.

Closing my lids, I search inside myself, aware of the flip of emotions, the raging battle between sadness and joy. In my mind's eye, I hold a feeling in front of me, examine it for the dreary yet splendid thing it is.

"I feel my pulse beating, telling me I'm alive."

I *am* among the living. Like the calm after a storm, the great

Creator can still my soul, let it rejoice in the wonder of today.

Eyes remaining closed, I continue. "The afternoon's heat is slowly cooling down to another evening, bringing me relief."

As if words are a healing balm, I feel my body lower to a pleasant temperature.

Then, a divine being descends on me. I tremble from His power, feel my bones strengthen from His touch. And like a photo flashing across my mind, I view a giant eagle's wing opening, inviting, enfolding.

"I sense Elohim's presence, like the mighty wind during the storm in Green Meadow. He's beckoning me to hide beneath His wings and find safety there. I don't need to hide out of fear. He's the final place I run to. I belong to Him, and one of the ways He'll show His unconditional love is through Sam."

Silence.

When I straighten, I let my watery eyes open slowly and travel to Shea's. Where did all of that come from?

Elohim.

There is no one but Elohim.

No one to praise.

No one to revere.

No one to be.

Who am I?

I am nothing without Him. And yet I am chosen by His grace.

Shea laughs heartily. "Your groom is ready for you."

I avert my gaze toward the sanctuary where Sam waits. Realizing I haven't let go of the hem of my gown, I charge forward. When I catch up to Alexis and Mom, I shout out to them, my voice spilling with happiness. "Come on, already! It's time!"

Time to transition from *what if* to what is and what will become.

Time to live the life I've been given.

I am soon to be Sam's wife. I am a daughter of the King. I am beautifully and wonderfully made.

I skip along the ground and lift my face up to the sky so the sun can burn away my fears.

AT THE BACK of the sanctuary, Dad smiles while leaning on a cane. "There you are, dazzling Pero. I was beginning to wonder if you were getting cold feet."

"Never." I hook my arm through his. A couple hundred Lesaries sit ahead of me. From the stage, a guitar softly plays a song I wrote.

Coming home, coming home, coming home.

Never have those words felt more true!

Alexis strung lights along the walls of the sanctuary and above the stage where Sam stands. From my angle, under the twinkling lights, he shines like a star, spectacular in all his brightness. He shifts on his feet, as if he's nervous, but as soon as his gorgeous brown eyes land on mine, he stiffens.

I sense more than see the crowd turning their heads toward me.

Dad leans near my ear. "Ready?"

"Yes, Pitar." The Old English word for *dad* is reserved for the most special of occasions, and this one beats them all.

For each slow step, I'm ready to catch Dad if he were to fall. Mom and Alexis made it to the front row where they stand to honor the bride, the rest of the room following their lead. I hear whispered words from the crowd. *Radiant. Blessed. Chosen.* I believe each of their proclamations, owning my place here among the Lesaries. With open arms, I accept who Elohim made me to be, love who He'll transform me into tomorrow.

Life is beautiful.

As we stagger down the aisle, Dad leans on me like I did on

him when I was a young girl, the two of us searching for a steady heartbeat as we stumbled through life. I steal glances at Sam, unable to get enough of his face. He's not the emotional type, yet tears surface, his face scrunched as if holding a torrent.

When I reach Sam's side, Shea recites. "Who gives this woman to be married to this man?"

Dad clears his throat. "She gives herself with the blessing of her two fathers and two mothers. The groom has paid the dowry."

We'd agreed to combine both the Lesarien and American traditions for the ceremony. Sam had "purchased" me by returning my heart from Henry, and he'd also paid a dowry to Alexis, Matthew, and Bahar. They had refused his generosity, saying this was an unusual situation since I hadn't been raised by Alexis, but he'd insisted on following tradition, blessing our parents financially to reflect the overflow of blessings he'd received.

Dad didn't leave Carper out of the picture when he said my two fathers blessed me to be married. Even though Carper had left me, he gave his approval beforehand. I may never see my blood dad again, yet I cherish his favor.

Sam and I join hands, the same spark igniting at every touch. After we exchange vows and rings, the Lesaries follow their tradition, saying in unison,

We are witnesses. May Yahweh bless your wife, building your house like Rachel and Leah built Israel's. Let your house be like that of Judah's, with offspring from Yahweh.

The Lesaries gather around our parents, lay hands on them, and bless them.

Let Elohim's name be famous in Origo. Sam and Pero's

future children will restore your family and sustain you as you grow older, for they love you.

How precious it is to witness the beauty of Elohim's people in unity!

The ceremony over, the Lesaries leave the sanctuary, taking turns giving me and Sam hugs and congratulations. Even Shea gives us space for a goodbye before the future celebration. I agreed to follow the Lesarien custom in this way too, yet now that we're about to depart, a piece of me wishes I'd suggested we blast off for a honeymoon together.

But there is wonder in the waiting for Sam's return.

I fold into his embrace, soaking in his woodsy smell, the comfort of my face against the crook of his neck. "How long will you be gone?"

"I'll prepare a place for you. I guess it depends on how many rooms you want in our house."

"Many." I lift my head to look directly at him. "I'd love plenty of space for whoever Elohim brings our way."

"You realize it could take me up to a year for something big. Maybe longer."

"Then one room is enough."

He rests his forehead against mine. "I'll do anything for you."

I close my eyes. I'd wait for a decade if that's what it took to be a recipient of such love. "Come quickly, Sam. All I want is you."

"You know I will."

"Even so," I whisper, "come."

He lifts my chin with a finger and lingers there. "Elohim's Spirit will remain with you. He'll go before you and encourage you. Don't be afraid of His power within you."

"I'm not afraid." Yet my voice trembles as he leans forward, sweeping me into a passionate kiss.

When he lets go, I stumble for a moment, embracing the way his nearness saps out my strength. It's okay to be weak. It's okay his return will find me in a state of dependence on the Spirit. In fact, I'll join all of Creation—the stinging rain, the forceful wind, the throbbing sun. We will groan together, eager for Sam's return.

For some, goodbye's forever. Not so with Sam. He may not be immortal, as he once claimed, but he promised to return, and Sam never breaks a promise.

After several quick kisses, him retreating more between each one, he squeezes my hand.

I yank him toward me for a last kiss. When I let him go, he leaves, turning around for another look with every few steps he takes toward the sanctuary's exit.

Blasted Lesarien customs! Yet, I'd agreed to this. Not because I'm eager for my favorite man to leave, but because this is another demonstration of his love for me. He's building a home for us, a place for me to belong.

The Spirit whispers, *Come.*

I, the bride, say, *Come.*

Singing out, my voice echoes off the sanctuary's walls. He runs, searching for a place we'll call our home. Can he hear my song? Does it spur him on?

When you lead me by still waters, you restore my soul.
Surely goodness and your mercy cover me.
I'm running after you.
Won't let any fear in my way.
I'm running after you.
Coming home, coming home, coming home.

My mind echoes with his tender voice, telling me he's coming back. Yet it sounds quieter, as if he hears my lullaby and holds onto the hope that he'll soon be on his way.

I close my eyes with my pendant in my fist, the one I love most out of view.

But not forever.

EPILOGUE
PERO

A mighty shout—similar to the one that knocked down Moon City's walls—vibrates off the houses.

"What's going on out there?" Mom asks.

I stay focused on my task of scrubbing lunch dishes. "Probably another race."

"In the late afternoon?" Mom heads toward the front window. "The sun will melt them all."

I've been living at Mom and Dad's since Sam left eight months prior. The days have flown by as I've filled them with activities, yet each morning, I ask Elohim, "Will he come today?" I try to avoid my mind retreating to worst-case-scenarios, that Sam got eaten by a wild animal or died of dehydration on his own. No news is good news, right?

"Pero?"

It takes a few seconds to recognize the lace of panic in Mom's tone. Or is that excitement?

I set the plate down, drying my hands on a towel. "What is it?"

"Pero!" She rushes to the front door, opens it wide, then charges outside.

I'm left in a puddle of confusion. Shouts continue, sentences from the voices becoming more coherent.

"He's here!"

"Sam's returned!"

"Where's Pero?"

A surge of heat travels through my body. My heartbeat races as I run outside where a parade of men carries one man on their shoulders.

Part of me begs to turn back, brush my hair, put on some makeup, but here I am with wrinkled hands from soapy water and an apron tied around my waist. I can at least get rid of the apron. Briskly walking forward, I untie it from the back, then throw it aside. I rush to the edge of the mob.

It's there that I wait.

When he sees me, he asks for the men to set him down. The crowd parts ways, as if creating a path through the Red Sea, leading straight to me.

I pause, embracing the stillness as he stands before me. To experience the deep and unfathomable love settling between, around, and inside us. The shouts dissipate, respecting this silence, allowing the power of our bond to penetrate the present.

"I'm here to bring my bride home," he says in a low voice. "I prepared a place for you with many rooms. Everything I've built is yours."

An overpowering sense of grace floods through me. I'm being drowned in his desire for me, his drive to make me his own. Who am I that he would humble himself before me? That he would become like a servant all in the name of love?

Covering my mouth with my hands, I cry.

He covers me with his wings, and under the shelter of his strength, I am made whole.

When the tears subside, his arms still holding onto me tight, he whispers in my ear. "Even though it's the Lesarien custom, I won't make you consummate here in one of these houses."

I kiss his cheek, refusing to let him go. "I don't care where we do it, as long as we get to."

He growls low, then squeezes me tighter.

Finding courage, I grab his hand, then pull him toward home. Yes, the house belongs to my parents, but do I care at this point?

"Come on, Sam."

His eyes are hungry, brows raised, feet willingly obeying as I drag him to the only place I want us to go.

"Let's consummate our marriage." I make my voice carry. "Did you hear me? We're having a party!"

The men cheer.

"Just so we're clear," I say. "My husband is the only one invited."

They whoop, slapping Sam's back along the way.

"Have fun!" Dad calls.

I glare at him, my face blushing, then shrug and laugh along.

"We'll find somewhere else to stay tonight!" Mom yells above the voices.

The crowd roars with laughter, then applauds my parents.

I have to admit, I kind of like these Lesarien traditions. Why not honor the joining of two becoming one? We'll still have privacy and the chance to celebrate our official marriage the next day before heading to our new home. Besides, I have the rest of my life to enjoy the house built for us.

Mmm. So grateful.

With a smile on my lips, I close the front door behind us.

DID YOU ENJOY THE BOOK?

One of the best ways you can support an author is by leaving a review. Please consider rating or sharing your experience of Meadow's Curse by visiting https://amzn.to/4103Hpc or scanning the QR code below.

Thank you!

DISCUSSION QUESTIONS

1. In the beginning of the story, Sam asks Elohim if it's the right time to contact Pero. How could waiting to start a relationship be beneficial? Describe a time when God asked you to wait. How did you feel in the process?

2. Pero has been through many trials, causing her to fear stepping out in faith and answer Sam's call. How have past difficulties enabled to or prevented you from taking a next step of faith?

3. When Cathena appears right after Sam's prayer for his "Eve," he wonders if she's the right one for him. Have you ever wondered if someone or something in front of you is an answer to prayer? How do you know this is from God?

4. Pero finds Dr. Carper in a lab, but she also discovers more about what he did to her mom in the past. How would you respond to such news? When is it worth it to forgive someone who hurt you or a loved one?

5. Quickly after Sam and Pero's reunion, Sam wanted to create boundary rules for their relationship. Why are boundaries a good idea when in a relationship? What rules would you make when dating your future spouse?

6. In the book of Ruth from the Bible, Ruth's mother-in-law advises that Ruth lay at Boaz's feet while he's sleeping so that he might take care of her family. Why can it be hard to humble ourselves for the sake of helping others?

7. Pero finds out that Henry stole her heart and must find him to request he return it. Have you ever regretted letting someone steal a piece of your heart? Who or what could help restore your pain from past break-ups? Is the idea of someone breaking or stealing your heart a big deal? Why or why not?

8. By entering what if, Pero can alter her past. Given a similar opportunity, would you alter your history? Why or why not? How might changing past decisions give you a different future?

9. Dr. Carper ends up walking away from Pero. Has someone you love ever abandoned you? What were your feelings regarding the situation? Who could you reach out to if you needed to talk through hurts?

10. According to biblical and Jewish scholars, one of the Israelites' customs was for the groom to leave and build a house for his bride. Similarly, Jesus left to prepare "many rooms" for his church, also commonly referred to as the bride of Christ. Have any of your morals or traditions pointed toward the need for a savior? Have you invited Jesus to rescue you from your shortcomings and pains and hold your heart? If not, what obstacles might be holding you back?

ACKNOWLEDGMENTS

The third book in the series is done! But not without the support of an incredible team behind the scenes.

Extraordinary critique group, I wouldn't be publishing my third book without you: Donald W. White, Heidi Gaul, Karen Barnett, Christina Suzann Nelson. You all give me the best laughs a person could ask for. And you care so deeply. Thank you!

A special thanks to Karen Grunst for continual calls, prayers, and reads. Whatever book you bought this week, I guarantee I bought it, too. We're so in sync! Love you. Can't wait to meet you in person someday!

Eric, you are a good man and an abundant blessing from God. You're my Sam. What a privilege to do life with you! P.S. Thanks for patiently teaching me a science lesson. Anything I didn't get right about Carper's experiment isn't your fault. It's just me trying to combine science with fantasy.

Matthew Bollmann, thanks for the rocket launcher idea.

"Earls Girls are tough. Earls Girls are strong. Earls Girls never give up, never give up." Haven the brave'n, you may have read more books than I did this year. I'm so proud of you. Sadie girl, your daily cartwheels inspire me to practice my writing until I improve, then practice some more.

To the bookstores who support me as a local author: Abe from Browser's Bookstore and Kevin from Willamette Christian Supply. Your advocacy doesn't go unnoticed.

My church family, I'm so grateful to have you in my life. Thanks for supporting me.

To the Christ Church leadership team, my dear friends. Your care means so much to me and Eric.

To Corvallis, because you make a college town look *real* good. Who wouldn't want to live where you can watch a two-time Olympic gold-medal gymnast do flips; listen to renown jazz musicians on a Friday night; eat the world's best pupuserias from the Saturday market; or ride a bike while passing cute robots and a no-drama llama? Go Beavs!

Readers, your virtual letter responses are so precious to me. Thank you for being an incredible part of my community. Onwerto and koach to you.

ABOUT THE AUTHOR

Best-selling, award-winning author **Amy Earls** writes fiction that explores intersections between life issues and faith. A college advisor, she holds a master's degree in education for adult learners, with an emphasis on writing. Amy lives in Oregon's Willamette Valley with her husband and two daughters.

Learn more about Amy, her virtual letters, and free offers at www.amyearls.com.